CAMERON 4

A NOVEL BY

JADE JONES

www.jadedpub.com

TO BE NOTIFIED OF NEW RELEASES, CONTESTS, GIVEAWAYS,

AND BOOK SIGNINGS IN YOUR AREA, TEXT **BOOKS** TO **44144**

1

Cameron stared at her reflection in the seventy-two-inch double vanity bathroom mirror. The dim lighting reflected off her cinnamon skin, and added a glow to her even complexion. Her brown hair fell an inch above her small shoulders, and a tattoo of her son's name covered the dime-sized scar near her collar bone from where she'd been shot. It was a painful reminder of all she had endured over the last few months.

Cameron released a sigh and turned her head from left to right, never removing her eyes from her reflection. Once again it was time for a change.

August Alsina's *"Downtown"* played on repeat in the master bedroom. The pungent aroma of marijuana filled both the bedroom and its connected bathroom. Justin was in daycare, and that was the only time Jude ever smoked. He'd been blowing more than usual lately due to the stress and finances.

Several months ago Jude had proposed to Cameron in hopes that one day they'd have a big wedding, and live a carefree life together where bills were paid on time and expenses could be afforded. Business was dwindling at Cameron's boutique, and income was becoming less and less by the month. Soon the couple would no longer be able to pay rent for the decent two-bedroom house in Richmond Heights. Something had to give.

Cameron grabbed the cutting scissors off the counter and proceeded to snip inches from her beautiful locks. After damn near all of her hair was inside the above counter bowl sink, she reached for the L'Oreal hair dye kit.

No one told me life would be this way...

I swear nobody told me...

Guess this is the game we chose to play...

Crazy how it's always been the same...

The mellow song's lyrics filled the 12x12 bedroom as Arizona kush filled Jude Patterson's lungs. Massaging, his temples he scrolled through his cellphone's contacts log. *My next move gotta be my best move*, he thought to himself. Shit had been really slow since his release from prison, and understandably his funds weren't the same.

Jude worked as a part time temp at a factory earning pennies—nothing like the big money he saw in the car business. Although, what he did was illegal and unwarranted, Jude raked in more money than he knew what to do with...and now he couldn't even afford an engagement ring for his girl.

With limited options, Jude tapped his cousin's name and hit the call button. Abel Soden—known by most as simply "Aso" was a year older than Jude and moved to Georgia several years ago, claiming that he needed better "opportunities". He always had some type of connection or plug when it came to making money, and with his brother gone Jude had no one else to turn to.

Aso answered on the third ring. "What's up, blood?" He turned down the Rich Homie Quan mixtape so that he could hear. "What's been good with you? We ain't chopped it up in a minute."

Jude wasted no time getting to business. "Shit, a nigga been on lock. I just got out a few months ago."

Aso already knew that, but he figured Jude didn't need to know that he did. Besides, it was neither here nor there. "Damn, bro. Well I'm glad to see you out and about now."

"I know, man. But look, I need somethin' to shake, straight up," Jude told Aso. "My pockets ain't how they used to be, fam...I know you be havin' ya hand in all types of shit so I thought I'd hit you up," he explained. "You know I ain't the type of nigga to ask for shit...but without my bruh, I'm lightweight lost. A nigga don't know what the fuck to do...or what direction to go."

It was Jude's first time admitting it, and as much as it hurt to say, it was true. His older brother Jerrell had led him to the money and virtually placed it in his hand. Now that his guidance was gone Jude had to come up with his own beneficial means of making cash.

Aso sighed in disappointment after the mention of Jerrell. He hated to hear that his cousin was getting the shitty end of the stick. For years Jude had been on top, holding it down, and gaining respect as a young nigga known to get money. It was fucked up how life could change in the blink of an eye.

"Yeah, I heard about that shit, man. I'm sorry to hear that," Aso said, offering his sincerest condolences. "You know that was the nigga. He done put some money in everybody's pockets at one time or another. All the real niggas gettin' taken out the game way too early. It's fucked up."

"Hell yeah…but it ain't shit else I can do but live and try to make him proud. Anyway, tell me you got somethin' for me to get into," Jude said, changing the sensitive subject. He still hadn't fully healed from his brother's death. "You already know I don't mind gettin' my hands dirty," he continued. "I'm finna get married and shit…I gotta lil' son of my own now. These nickels and dimes ain't cuttin' it. I need some action, bruh."

Jude's dark eyes settled on the master bathroom's closed door. He didn't want Cameron to overhear his conversation. His pride would be damaged if she knew he was asking for help especially since he was a nigga who never ever fixed his mouth up to ask for favors. Everything Jude ever owned he had worked hard for and he took immense pride in that.

Aso blew out air and ran a hand over his softly brushed waves. He resembled Jude with his light skin and pretty boy looks. Aso's piercing hazel eyes were his best feature. His body was tattooed completely from his neck to his torso. There was a small crescent-shaped scar underneath his left eye from a fight over two years ago.

Aso talked to Jude on his cellphone while watching a thick redbone make her way inside the downtown salon he was parked across the street from. His girl had called him thirty minutes ago and told him to pick her up, but it was obvious she was still inside running her mouth because she had yet to come out.

"You know I wouldn't 'een be doin' this shit if you wasn't fam, but I know you'd look out if the shoe was on the other foot," Aso finally said. "I can't really say too much over the phone but what you need to do is leave that decrepit ass city and bring ya ass down South. If you really serious about makin' some money I might have somethin' for you—after I holla at my peoples, of course," he quickly added.

Jude took a short pull on his L. "Leave Cleveland?" he repeated, with a lungful of smoke. "I ain't never put much thought into that shit." He released the smoke and a few dry, hacking coughs.

"Man, ain't shit up there, nigga," Aso told him.

He watched as his girl, Lana finally emerged from the salon with her twenty-two inch mane curled to perfection. Traffic seemed to slow down when she stepped out. Lana Princeton was definitely a looker with her smooth and radiant chocolate skin and coke bottle figure. Her waist was almost nonexistent, and her ass sat up high and round on full display for bitches to hate and men to salivate over. Lana loved the attention though. As a matter-of-fact she was one of the biggest attention whores Aso had ever known.

Lana switched extra hard in her $2700 Alexander McQueen dress as she made her way over towards Aso's parked silver Maserati GranCabrio. He spoiled her ass like crazy even though she was undeserving of the shit half the time.

Chuckling, Aso said, "You need to do like 'Bron and take talents to the South." Since Lana was about to join him he decided to wrap up the conversation. If it was one thing he couldn't stand, it was to have a bitch in his personal business. "Look, fuck with me cuz. Hit me when you ready to make that come up. I got you. Don't worry about shit. Just lemme know when you ready, aight? I'm out cuz." Aso disconnected the call just as Lana climbed inside. Her Pink Friday perfume greeted him before she did.

Meanwhile, Jude sat staring at the home screen on his cellphone. Reality was closing in, and he had to make a change not only for himself but for his family as well.

After climbing out of the king sized panel bed, Jude smashed the roach into the plastic ashtray on the nightstand and joined Cameron in the bathroom. She blow-dried her hair without a care in the world. Obviously, life wasn't stressing her out as much as it was him.

Cameron looked at Jude's reflection in the bathroom mirror. "You like it?" she asked.

His eyes grew big. He neither liked nor disliked it. "It's...different...," he struggled to say.

Cameron giggled. "It'll look better when it's styled," she promised.

Jude slowly walked up behind her, and wrapped his chiseled arms around her waist. Justin had put a little meat on her bones but thankfully it was in all the right places. Cameron's curves were on full display in a lace camisole with matching boy shorts.

"What you think about movin' out of Ohio?" Jude asked.

Finally tearing her gaze away from the mirror, Cameron turned around and faced Jude. He desperately needed a lineup, and his dreads to be re-twisted. Unfortunately, their finances were taking a major toll on him. Most nights he stayed up and lay in bed while Cameron slept soundlessly beside him. Because of that, small bags rested underneath his usually vibrant eyes.

"I can think about it all day long but it's not like we can afford that," Cameron answered. She was already struggling to hold onto the boutique that she worked so hard to get.

"But what if we could?" Jude asked her. "Would you?"

Cameron turned around and raked a hand through her new short, blonde hair while looking over her reflection. "I don't know," she answered truthfully. "I've been living in Cleveland all my life. It's all I know."

"But all you've been talkin' about for the last couple of weeks was makin' a change," Jude reminded her. "And Atlanta might be that change, babe."

"First of all, I was talking about my hair, boy," Cameron laughed.

Jude placed his arms on the bathroom counter so that Cameron was trapped in front of him. "But I'm talkin' 'bout somethin' bigger than a haircut," he said. There was no trace of humor on his handsome face. "If the opportunity presented itself would you be down to start over with me in ATL?" His intense gaze remained locked on hers through the mirror as he waited to receive an honest answer.

Cameron turned around and faced Jude again. He towered over her by a few inches and made her feel so protected and secure. "I'll follow you any and everywhere," she admitted. "You know that."

Jude leaned down and pressed his lips against

Cameron's forehead. "I really needed that reassurance," he told her.

"Why?" Cameron asked, disregarding his romantic gesture. "Are you planning on moving?" Her tone dripped with sarcasm yet little did she know how serious her man actually was. "What about the boutique?"

"You could sell that space and get the money for it. Hell, it ain't like we can't use it."

"And just what's in Atlanta?" Cameron asked. She finally noticed how serious he was about the move.

Jude's jaw muscle tensed as he focused on Cameron. Since he couldn't keep it real with her for fear that she'd be disappointed in him, he instead said, "Opportunities..."

Cameron stood on her tip toes and kissed Jude's full lips. They were perfect. Not too thick. Not too small. "Well, we've got an hour before I have to go and pick up Justin...," she gently nibbled on his bottom lip. "So why don't you handle this *opportunity* in the bathroom?"

Jude's dick immediately jerked awake. "Shit, say no more..." Backing her against the sink, he lifted her up and placed her on the counter. "So you wanna be handled, huh?" he asked.

Cameron pulled her lace cami over her head, and tossed it to the rustic bathroom tile. "I do."

Jude stepped out of his Adidas basketball shorts. "Ain't this how the first one was made?" he asked, referring to their son.

Cameron giggled. "I can't remember...why don't

you remind me?"

Jude scoffed. "You wanna play? Bend dat ass over."

Like a naughty school girl obeying her instructor, she leaned over the double vanity and tooted her round ass upward. For several seconds Jude simply admired the back view. It didn't matter how many times they made love or how long they'd been together; Cameron would always be sexy as hell to him. It'd gotten to the point where he didn't even want to look at another broad because they didn't have shit on what he had at home.

Grabbing a handful of her soft, plump ass, Jude slid inside Cameron from behind. She shivered upon his entrance, and placed one hand on his hip and the other on the bathroom mirror.

"Oh my goodness," she moaned in pleasure.

The faint sound of music and the wet noises from Jude slipping in and out of Cameron's slippery pussy were the only things that could be heard.

Jude leaned downward and placed delicate kisses along her spine before running the tip of his tongue along the nape of her neck. That always drove Cameron crazy.

Jude draped an arm around her neck from behind as he watched her watch them through the mirror. "You see how fuckin' good we look together?" he asked. "You was put on this earth for me." Jude kissed her earlobe. "Tell me again you'll follow me wherever."

Cameron's cheeks flushed bright red as she felt a powerful orgasm approaching. "Shit!" she cried out. "I'll follow you anywhere!"

Jude smiled in satisfaction and resumed tearing that ass up from the back. Cameron's c-cup breasts swung back and forth over the bowl sink with each stroke he inflicted.

"I ain't comin' til' you come, bay," Jude told her. Cam's wetness drenched his curved dick as he dug deep, slid out halfway and plowed back inside. "Damn, this pussy was made for this dick. You know what? Fuck this sink shit. Let's take this to bed."

Before Cam could either agree or disagree, Jude swept her up in his arms and carried her inside the bedroom before tossing her onto the panel bed. Her nude body flopped a few times before she anxiously sat up on her knees and took Jude's glistening dick in her warm mouth.

Jude moved his mid-length dreads out the way so that he could watch the show. When he could no longer contain himself, he pushed Cameron onto her back and dived inside her wetness.

"We keep fuckin' like this we gon' be makin' more babies." Perspiration rolled off Jude's forehead and dripped onto Cameron's upper lip.

She licked it off. "That'd be on you," she smiled. Her legs tightened around his waist.

"This pussy shouldn't be so good," Jude said, leaning down to kiss Cameron—

KSSHHHHH!

The sudden sound of glass shattering caused the two to jump up. The earsplitting sound had come from downstairs.

2

"What the hell was that?!" Cameron yelled, snatching the sheets around her bosom. They lived in a fairly decent neighborhood where crime was minimal. Surely no one could have been foolish enough to break into someone's house in broad daylight—then again, the world was a crazy place.

Jude hopped out the bed, snatched on a pair of sweatpants, and grabbed his Nine from the closet.

Cameron started to climb out the bed, but Jude immediately stopped her. "Naw, you stay up here. As a matter of fact, call the police."

Cameron's heart pounded inside her chest, and it took her brain several seconds to register what he had just said. Jude cautiously exited the bedroom as she scurried to the dresser for her cellphone. Her fingers trembled as she dialed 9-1-1. Right before she hit the call button, Gucci Mane's *"Darker"* blared through the small speaker on Jude's cellphone. The unexpected call caused her to jump once more. Naturally, Cameron's nerves were on edge.

Downstairs, Jude investigated the loud crash while holding firmly onto his piece. Instead of finding a ski-masked intruder, he found a red brick lying in the center of the family room. The opulent bay window had been smashed to pieces.

Great. Another mothafuckin expense we can't afford, Jude thought. He figured the attack had to have been kids or a hate crime. Either way, he wouldn't be able to sleep comfortably knowing his family could be in danger.

Upstairs, Cameron gradually made her way over towards the night table where Jude's cellphone continued to ring.

All of a sudden, Jude stepped back inside the bedroom. The aggravation was evident on his face as he walked past Cameron to answer his phone. Jude was so preoccupied with everything going on that he didn't even notice the call was from a private number.

"Hello?" Jude answered with irritability in his tone.

No response.

"Hello?!"

Cameron stood by with the ivory sheet wrapped around her naked body.

"Yo? Hello?" Jude barked into the mouthpiece.

CLICK!

The mysterious caller disconnected the call.

"The fuck?" Jude said, staring at the home screen on his cell.

The screeching sound of a car skirting off caused Cam and Jude to race toward the bedroom window. A silver Toyota Camry burned rubber as it disappeared around the corner, leaving behind a thin gust of smoke.

***

Aso and Lana cruised through Midtown with Jay Z and Rick Ross' *"Fuck With Me You Know I Got It"* on full blast. One would've assumed Lana was on her way to a photo-shoot by the way she was caking on makeup in the passenger seat when in all actuality they were just on their way to lunch.

Since work kept Aso preoccupied for most days, he tried to devote a little quality time to Lana every now and then.

Aso reached over and lowered the volume. "Aye, why you puttin' all that bullshit on ya face when we just goin' out to eat?"

Lana sucked her teeth but kept her gaze locked on her compact mirror. She was so sick and tired of his ass, and the only reason she stayed with him was because he spoiled her. Little he did know, she was sexing someone else while he was busy making money.

"Don't tell me you turned my song down just to start some shit," Lana said.

Aso shook his head. He and Lana fought like cats and dogs but he loved her black ass. "I think my peoples finna move out here," he said, changing the subject. "They up in Ohio right now."

Lana applied a thick coat of MAC's nude lipstick. "And? What the fuck does that have to do with me?" For her to come from a wealthy background Lana could be ghetto as hell at times. The fact that Aso also spoiled her didn't help much either.

"'Cuz they're more than likely gonna be stayin' in the townhome. And I told you 'bout that mouth. I'ma stop warnin' ya ass and just start slappin' you in yo' shit."

Lana brushed his meaningless threat off. "But that's where my parents stay when they come in town," she complained. "How're you just going to move someone else in their place?"

Aso tore his eyes off the road long enough to look at his girl like she was crazy. "Lana, you barely like them mothafuckas. Shit, it wasn't even that long ago when you were talkin' 'bout havin' 'em killed for an inheritance. Now you give a fuck where they stay when they come in town?"

Lana shrugged as if having her dear old parents murdered wasn't a big deal. She'd sell her soul to the devil for a pair of red bottoms.

"Look, if my peoples decide not to come down then—" Aso's sentence was cut off by the sound of his iPhone ringing. He answered immediately after seeing Jude's name flash across the screen. "Damn, bruh. That was quick. You made ya decision that fast?"

"Man, it ain't shit but trouble for me out here," Jude said. "Whatever you got, count me in."

***

Four days after the window incident, Cameron sat in the tall unkempt grassy area in front of her parents' flat headstones. It was a sunny day, peaking in at a beautiful 79 degrees. There were plenty other things Cameron could've enjoyed doing that day, but instead she chose to pull the weeds from around their headstones while having a one-sided conversation with nothing but their hollow shells resting underneath the earth.

"Jude wants to move to Atlanta...," she said to no one in particular. She picked a few pieces of grass off her gray maxi dress. "I'm not really feeling it...but it's not like there's really much going on here..." Cameron paused. "I don't know...sometimes I wish I had ya'll here to guide me—tell me what to do when I have no idea what decision is right."

A slight breeze blew through her blonde Pixie cut. It was a lot cuter now that it had been styled, and was reminiscent of Barbadian singer, Rihanna's short haircut.

"Sometimes I'm not always sure what's right and what's wrong. Sometimes I don't know what the best decision to make is...and honestly it hurts and stresses me the hell out sometimes. It's frustrating. Life is like a maze, you know? You gotta go through the right passages to make it out okay. But it's so easy to make a wrong turn." Tears formed in Cameron's brown eyes. She wiped them away before they could fall and forced a smile. "I guess I gotta bump my head a couple times before I get it right, huh?" Cameron wanted to believe she could hear her mother laughing with her, and although that was impossible the thought was comforting.

Cameron looked in the direction of the parking lot. Jude and Justin were waiting inside the truck so that she could have her moment of solitude.

"At first I was angry," she continued. "I was angry at ya'll for dying. I was angry that you left me all alone in this cold, cruel world. I was angry at having to be moved from group home to group home...I was just...angry. I felt alone," Cameron confessed. "I wanted that affection—I needed the love I felt I never got." Tears spilled over her lower lids but she didn't bother wiping them away that time. "I thought Silk, and stripping, and money could fill that void...but it didn't. It only made it worse." Cameron smiled. "But luckily my superman came to save me. And since he didn't give up on me I can't give up on him. I can't give up on us." She kissed two fingers and placed them on each of her parents' headstones. "I love ya'll. Watch over me and continue to guide me...'cuz I really need it."

***

One week later, they packed their belongings inside of a 26-foot rental truck and made the eleven-hour drive to Georgia. Initially, Cameron was skeptical about the speedy, impulsive move. However, Jude set her at ease by assuring her that his cousin had a job for him that offered great "benefits". Cameron had no idea about the specifics, and the details were even a little sketchy to Jude but he wasn't really sweating it. He'd done everything from slinging dope to insurance fraud. He was desperate and would do whatever it took to take care of his family.

3

Jude, Cameron, and Justin left Cleveland, Ohio at approximately 5 a.m., and didn't make it to Atlanta, Georgia until 6:30 p.m. The ride was smooth up until they got on 75 and got caught in the rush hour traffic.

By the time they pulled up to a gorgeous 3 bedroom 2 ½ bathroom townhome located in Midtown, they were tired, their muscles were stiff, and they were hungry. On top of that, Justin's fussiness had given Cameron a headache. Not accustomed to being in a car for long he practically cried the whole ride there. He'd fallen asleep for twenty minutes only to wake back up and resume.

Seeing the beautiful townhome was enough to make Cameron temporarily forget about all her problems. She cheered up instantly when she how lovely the neighborhood was. Atlanta was definitely a sight to see. The Georgia aired even smelled different.

Jude parked the massive moving truck along the curb and hopped out to greet the tall, slender guy standing at the foot of a home's staircase. At first glance he reminded Cameron of Young Money rapper, Tyga. Based on their strong resemblance anyone could tell that he and Jude were related.

Justin whined in Cameron's embrace. "Ssh. Please calm down for mommy. You want me to take you to Chuck E. Cheese still, right?" she asked, trying to pacify with kiddie entertainment.

"No!" Justin cried, violently shaking his little head. Yes and no seemed to be the only words in his vocabulary.

Cameron and Jude had spoiled him so much that he was borderline bratty. Nearly two years old, Justin was proving to be a handful especially for a new mother.

Jude and Aso dapped each other up before embracing each other in a brotherly hug. Jude was a student at OSU in Columbus, Ohio the last time they saw each other. During that time Jude was only working as a salesman at Jerrell's car lot, and selling green here and there to his fellow students.

"What's good with you, man? A nigga done got swole out here I see," Aso joked before playfully jabbing Jude's peck. His prison muscles bulged through the fitted t-shirt.

Just then Cameron stepped out the truck with Justin in tow.

Jude chuckled. "Shit, just maintainin'. Been hittin' that good ole gym as a stress reliever," he said. "How ya brother doin' tho?"

"He straight," Aso answered. "Nigga still on the run after that shootin' in Cleveland and shit. He been layin' low tho, keepin' himself preoccupied with work."

Jude wondered what Aso meant exactly by work, but he decided to hold his questions for later. Besides, Cameron and his son were making their way over towards them.

"Anyway," Jude continued. "I hate to rush but could you help a nigga unload a couple things so we can get settled? We're tired as all hell after that drive, man."

The sun beat down on Jude as they stood outside

in front of the townhome. The weather would definitely take some getting used to.

Aso blew a raspberry and waved him off. "Nigga, fuck all that. I got some people to handle that shit."

He turned towards the strung out looking older guys sitting on the next house's steps and snapped his finger at them. They were nonexistent a few seconds ago. Apparently, Jude had overlooked them. Leave it to Aso to pay some fiends to move in the furniture.

Like trained pets obeying their master, the addicts scurried towards the Budget truck.

"Cuz, you think it's safe havin' these mothafuckas move our stuff in?" Jude asked as he watched them anxiously get to work.

Aso placed a hand on Jude's shoulder and gave him a gold-fanged grin. "Man, they straight. But look, I got somebody you need to meet."

Cameron raised an eyebrow in skepticism after hearing the tail end of the conversation. "Who?" she asked.

Aso extended his hand. "You must be Cameron," he said, purposely ending the conversation before she heard too much.

Aso was thoroughly impressed with his cousin's taste. Cameron was bad as hell. The destroyed high waist jeans she wore hugged her shapely hips, accentuating every curve. Her neon yellow top revealed an ample amount of her toned tummy.

Damn, she fine than a mothafucka, Aso thought to himself. *Jude better keep his eye on this one.*

"I was just tellin' him that I wanted him to meet my boss," Aso explained. "We recently got an open position up at my job that I promised him." He squeezed Jude's shoulder.

"Yeah, you remember that whole thing about opportunities? Well this is it," Jude said. He was still holding back the fact that whatever his "job" was would be illegal. "Just trust me. Aight?"

Cameron gave Jude a suspicious look. She wanted to berate him for more details and reassurance, but now wasn't the time or the place. After all, it wasn't like they weren't already in Atlanta.

"Why don't you go and get settled inside," Jude told her. His eyes pled with her to just trust him.

Aso ruffled Justin's short, curly as he and Cameron walked past. When they were inside and out of earshot, Aso turned his attention back to Jude. "Come on, let's take a lil' ride."

Jude followed him to his Maserati and climbed into the passenger seat.

"Aye, don't scratch or scuff up shit!" Aso yelled to the bootleg movers before hopping in the driver's side.

***

Cameron carried her son on her hip as she carefully made her way through each and every room in the elegant three-story townhome. The house was much more updated than the one they'd just moved from.

Cameron's suspicions were on full alert. Certainly there was some type of stipulation to staying here...or was

Aso really that generous? *What's really going*, she asked herself.

"Excuse me, ma'am?" A raspy voice called out. "Where you want us to put this?"

The overwhelmingly stale scent of mustiness filled the home as two movers struggled to carry the egg white tufted sofa. Their grimy hands were getting dirt prints all over the expensive fabric.

Wrinkling her nose, Cameron pointed to an area in the sitting room. At the foot of the spacious room was a beautiful two story stone fireplace. The ornate built-ins accentuated the area and added a modern appeal.

Cameron was in love with the gorgeous property, but she only had one question: How the hell were they going to afford its expenses?

***

"It's just us now, and I'm finally down here," Jude said. "Give it to me straight, cuz. What's good?" He didn't make an eleven-hour drive only to be left in suspense.

Aso made a left turn on 12th street.

Jude took in the scenery as he patiently waited for a responsive.

"Aight, it's like this. So I'm fuckin' with this car biz now—and the shit's actually profitable."

"And what exactly do you do?"

"Steal whips," Aso said casually.

Jude tore his gaze away from the tall buildings and looked over at his cousin. For a second, he thought he had misheard Aso. "*Stealin' cars*?!"

"Nigga, this shit's much bigger than just stealin' cars though," Aso laughed. "It's a whole mothafuckin' operation, bruh. Real intricate."

Jude's interest was piqued. "Oh really?" he asked. "How so?"

Aso fired up a joint and took an aggressive pull before handing it to his younger cousin.

"Really though?" Jude chuckled, taking the tightly rolled joint.

"A nigga like me don't smoke blunts so I keep dem joints in rotation," Aso joked, reciting one of Wiz Khalifa's verses. "Anyway the shit's like this...My boss runs this million-dollar car theft ring. He's like a fence for the stolen property. He gets the orders and sends us to look for the cars. Sometimes we get multiple orders—which is why we could use some extra hands."

Jude toked on the joint a few times and handed it back to Aso. "Car theft ring?" he repeated skeptically. "I ain't never heard of no shit like that. How does it work?"

Aso sucked the loud into his lungs and then expelled it through his nostrils. The inside of his Maserati GranCabrio quickly became a gas chamber as the two men touched the sky.

"There's levels to this shit, man," Aso told him. "You got us—the members—what they call us—we steal the cars and shit. You gon' meet my patnah, Vado tonight too, by the way. And then you got the runners. They're the niggas who transport the vehicles. The ones who move the inventory around a lil', you know...keep the police detection down. And then you got the mufuckas who broker the cars and change the VINs. I'm sayin' bruh, this shit's big. We ship cars overseas to all types of got damn countries. But our main connect's in West Africa."

Jude's wispy eyebrows furrowed from confusion. "*West Africa*?!"

"Shit, hell yeah. West Africa's a big market for stolen cars. The demand for black market wheels is high as hell, bruh."

Jude tried to absorb as much info as he could while the greenery soothed him. "Damn," was all he could say. The weed had him stuck. "Cam would flip if she knew what was up."

Aso fired up a second joint. "Man, she ain't gotta know shit," he said, passing the L to Jude.

4

The sun was just beginning to set when Ericka brought her Toyota Camry to a slow creep on Jude and Cameron's street. Instead of seeing their Audi Q7 there was a burgundy 2011 Buick Lacrosse parked in their driveway. The second thing she noticed was that the bay window she'd broken had been replaced.

Ericka lowered the volume to Rihanna's "*Diamonds*" as she brought her car to a slow stop. She always put on her girl Rih whenever she prepared to turn up. The Barbadian bad girl empowered her in a sense.

Since Ericka's release, she'd gone right back to her old ways even though she promised correction officers, her lawyers, counselors—and even the judge—that she'd change. Femme-fatale was an understatement. Ericka Matthews put Jennifer Jason Leigh in "*Single White Female*" to shame. Jude was the object of her affection, and she wouldn't stop until she got back what she felt was rightfully hers.

Snatching the gears into park, Ericka stepped out the car. Her long butter pecan colored legs were the first thing to grab a man's attention. That was obvious when the realtor standing in Jude's front lawn broke his neck to look at her. He was a white, short chubby guy with thick framed glasses.

Ericka sashayed over towards him, immediately noticing the For Rent sign in his hand. She gripped her shoulder bag and tried to appear as sane as possible. With her angelic looks and sweet smile, no one would ever suspect her of being deranged.

Ericka's light skin tone hinted that she was obviously biracial. She had pouty pink lips, beautiful gray eyes, and curly sandy brown hair.

"Good evening," Ericka greeted in a sugary voice. "I was just coming to surprise my brother by stopping by," she lied. "Don't tell me they moved?"

The realtor pushed his glasses up on the bridge of his nose. "Moved out last night," he told her.

Ericka tried to mask her anger, but she felt her complexion slowly turning bright red. She'd stayed away a few weeks to let the window incident die down only to come back and discover that they'd moved.

"I know Jude's punk ass wasn't that scared of a little brick through his window," she muttered.

"Excuse me?" the realtor asked in puzzlement.

Ericka forced an artificial smile. "Oh nothing," she quickly said. She stepped closer to him in hopes that her sweet fragrance would entice him. "Look, I just came back home from the Air Force and I haven't been keeping in touch as much I should've been," she explained. "Is there any way you can help me out by giving me their new address?"

The realtor shook his head, obviously unsympathetic to her situation. "No can do," he said.

Ericka immediately dropped the phony act and allowed her attitude to surface. "What do you mean no can do? You can't give me my brother's new address?" Her tone raised a few octaves.

The realtor went from being attracted to Ericka to being intimidated by her in less than ten seconds. "I—I don't know it," he stuttered. "And even if I did I wouldn't be able to tell you that—"

Ericka stormed off before he could finish. She was seething mad as she dug inside her shoulder bag and pulled out a four-inch automatic switchblade. Without thinking twice, she stabbed his left Michelin tire, and ran the blade along the spotless burgundy paint.

EEERRRRRRRRR!

The screeching sound of metal on metal tore through the quiet evening air.

"Hey! What the hell are you doing?!" the realtor yelled.

By the time he ran over to his car to survey the damage Ericka was already inside of her own peeling off.

***

The Warehouse, located on the outskirts of the city, also doubled as a chop. The King—or simply referred to as "King"—ran one of the biggest advanced car theft rings in the nation. After having the vehicles stolen, he paid to get the VINs changed and fraudulent titles made. After all the "paperwork" was completed and the vehicle's history was erased, King had the cars placed in a shipping container to be sent overseas. His elaborate organization worked hard to make the shipments appear lawful. He'd even established relationships with several dealers in order to get the key cut by VIN directly. King also tossed some of Fulton County's finest a few stacks to help with his elaborate scheme. Everything ran smoothly and efficiently.

Jude was extremely impressed when he entered the warehouse used to temporarily store stolen vehicles. The inside was every mechanics dream. The warehouse/chop shop had a purple and silver theme. There was also a rotating circular stage in the center with two topless dancers performing. Rap music coupled with the sound of drills and machinery was music to Jude's ears. It reminded him of when he had his own car business and lived lavishly. His success seemed like a distant memory.

The brown-skinned dancer winked at Jude as soon they made eye contact. He pretended he didn't notice as he followed Aso towards a gang of guys standing beside a black 2013 Hennessey Venom GT Spyder. Jude had only seen the 1.1 million-dollar vehicle in magazines. He felt sorry for the motherfucker who once owned it.

"What's good with ya, fam?" Aso dapped up a few of the fellas before pointing to a short Vietnamese man. There was a tribal tattoo on the left side of his face similar to Mike Tyson's. Judging from his thuggish attire and bad boy swag he wasn't the average Asian man. "Jude, this my patnah, Vado I was tellin' you about."

Jude stepped forward and gave Vado a manly handshake. He was surprised by the 5"6 man's strength.

Got your main bitch on the handle, she dropping and popping no castles...

I'm smoking on gas like tobacco, I'm drinking on lean taste like Snapple...

In the VIP rolling a cord, passing out mollies to foreigns...

They popping them like they some skittles, 2 bitches one me, Malcolm in the middle...

Migos' "*Hanna Montana*" blared through the sport car's custom speakers. The two topless women danced on the rotating stage for no one in particular. They were there simply for entertainment purposes, not for tips.

"Come on, my boss wanna holla at you real quick," Aso told Jude.

***

Since Jude was out doing his thing with his cousin, Cameron decided to find something constructive to do with her time. The movers had finished unloading everything thirty minutes ago, and besides a few boxes that needed unpacking, everything was in order.

After feeding Justin and putting him to sleep it felt good to have some quality time for herself. Wearing a flag printed American Apparel t-shirt and acid washed denim shorts, Cameron stepped outside to get a breath of fresh of air. She was shoeless but the warm concrete felt good on her bare feet. The view of the city from the townhome was absolutely magnificent. She still couldn't believe she was actually in Atlanta, Georgia.

A year ago, I would've never thought I'd be here, Cameron thought to herself.

The sudden sound of a dog yelping grabbed her attention. She watched as a pretty dark-skinned female stepped out of her home two doors down. She was dressed casually in a leopard maxi skirt, white crop top and gladiator sandals. A lace headband was wrapped around her head.

The cream miniature schnauzer began barking at Cameron the moment he saw her. She never did like dogs and the disdain was obviously mutual.

"I'm sorry. He barks at everything and everyone. Don't take it personal," the young woman said before firing up a Newport.

"I won't," Cameron smiled.

"You just moved here?" the woman asked. She blew the smoke through her slightly parted lips.

"This evening," Cameron answered.

"I'm Rumor," she walked over to Cameron to shake her hand.

Rumor's hair was cut in a shoulder length asymmetrical bob. She instantly reminded Cameron of the actress Taral Hicks with her smooth chocolate skin and high cheekbones. She was pretty enough to be a video model.

"Cameron—or Cam for short. Whichever's cool."

"You from Georgia?"

"Ohio," Cameron answered.

Rumor scoffed. "Ohio? What's that like, the country?"

"I'm from Cleveland," Cameron told her. "It's very much the city...not as big as Atlanta...but far from being country."

The miniature schnauzer continued to yap until Rumor told him to shut the hell up. Surprisingly, he did. "You in school?" she asked Cameron.

"No. I graduated from CSU last year."

"Oh okay, cool. You moved down here by yourself?"

Cameron wondered if everyone in Georgia was equally as inquisitive as Rumor. "No. With my dude and my son."

Rumor smiled, revealing a pair of deep dimples. "What do you do?" she took another pull on the Newport.

Cameron shrugged. "I owned a little boutique back home but I sold the space before I moved down here," she explained. "I guess when I get situated and back on my feet I'll look into opening one down here. How about you?"

"I dance at Persuasion."

Figures, Cameron thought. Just the mere mention of stripping made her think about all the shit she'd gone through. Cameron had sworn it off...however, the thought of the easy money made returning seem very tempting.

"You make good tips?" Cameron asked.

Rumor nodded her head towards the townhome. "Section 8 damn sure wouldn't cover this shit," she retorted.

Cameron looked out at the city. "I used to dance," she admitted in a low tone.

"Ever thought about coming out of retirement?" Rumor asked. "You damn sure got the body for it," she said, looking Cameron's figure over.

"My dude wouldn't have that," she told her.

Rumor's schnauzer tugged on the leash. He was obviously bored with standing around listening to meaningless conversation. "Well, it was nice meeting you," she said. "I guess I'll see you around. Maybe we can hang out sometimes. It's always good to have a friend in a new city."

Cameron nodded her head in agreement. "That sounds cool."

Rumor made her way back towards her townhome. When she reached the foot of her stairs she turned towards Cameron. "It ain't nothing wrong with having your own money, Miss Cameron," she said.

Before Cameron could allow her words to sink in, Rumor disappeared inside of her home.

Cameron shrugged the statement off as she walked back inside her townhome. *She seems cool.*

***

Rumor tossed her house keys on the foyer accent table. She then removed Tigger—her miniature schnauzer's—leash and allowed him to roam freely. Pictures of her and her boyfriend, Calix donned the off white walls of the entryway. The sweet smell of incense burning greeted her senses the moment she walked further inside.

Rumor's cozy townhome was neat and organized. Not a decorative ornament was out of place. At first glance the home looked like it belonged to a normal happy couple...until Rumor walked through the kitchen and opened the door that led to the spacious garage area.

The room was completely dark since Rumor had taped cardboard over the garage door windows so that no one could look inside. The sound of labored breathing was the only thing that could be heard inside of the junky garage.

5

When Rumor flicked the light switch on she saw Calix lying in a fetal position with his arms and legs bound with cable wire. There was a thick piece of duct tape over his mouth. Dried blood covered his face from the four-day old gash on his forehead.

"Mmm," he groaned in pain with his eyes still shut tightly. The light bulb seemed twice as intense since he was used to being in total darkness.

Rumor slowly made her way over towards Calix. The heels of her gladiator sandals clicked against the filthy concrete. When she reached him she leaned over his body.

The putrid stench of urine filled the 16x18 garage. Calix had pissed himself at least five times since his imprisonment. He still wore the same outfit: a pair of True Religion jeans, a gray beater, and dirty white socks.

The afternoon Calix admitted to sleeping with her sister Roxie, Rumor had completely snapped. She smashed a $300 Neiman Marcus wine jug over his head, knocking him out instantly. While he lay unconscious and bleeding profusely from his head, Rumor dragged him inside the garage and tied his arms and legs together. Fighting pit bulls were treated better than Calix. Rumor kept him alive only so he could feel the same hurt and pain that he'd inflicted on her.

Rumor lit another cigarette as she stared at a weak Calix. "What's wrong baby?" she asked in the same tone one would use if speaking to a toddler.

Calix responded by making muffled noises.

Rumor heartlessly snatched the duct tape off his thick lips and he winced in pain. "I'm...dying...," he struggled to say.

Rumor sucked her teeth and rolled her eyes. "Boy, you ain't damn dying," she told him. "You're probably just hungry. Is that what it is?"

If Calix had enough strength he would've head-butted her crazy ass, but all he could do was lay feebly on the cold, hard garage floor. The hunger pains in his stomach were intolerable, and he was incredibly dehydrated.

Rumor took a pull on her cigarette and gently ran her fingers along his cheek. At twenty-seven, Calix Ramirez was fine as hell—on his good days. His caramel skin tone and short curly hair showed off his Dominican heritage. He was an average 5"10 with a slender, toned frame. Stubble had formed around his chiseled jawline and he smelled horribly.

"Mmm," Calix groaned in agony. He struggled to open his light brown eyes.

Without remorse, Rumor smashed the tip of the cigarette into his arm to put it out.

"*Gaaaahhhh!*" Calix cried out.

Rumor instantly covered his mouth so that the neighbors couldn't hear.

Tigger ran inside the smell garage, yapping the entire time. After he ran over to Calix he anxiously began licking his face. He was oblivious to the situation occurring in front of him.

Pain shot throughout Calix's entire body. The burning sensation immediately had him up and alert. "You fuckin' bitch!" he spat through Rumor's fingers.

Rumor hastily covered his mouth with the duct tape so that she wouldn't have to deal with anymore of his obscenities.

She slowly stood to her feet and snapped her finger. Tigger followed obediently at her heels as she exited the garage. Minutes later, Rumor returned with last night's cold picked over leftovers.

Kneeling by Calix's side, she peeled the tape off his mouth, this time less aggressively. "You hungry?" she asked sweetly before digging her bare hands into the plate of food.

Before Calix could respond, Rumor viciously stuffed the food inside his oral cavity. He choked on the remnants of dinner, and struggled swallowing it.

"Better?" Rumor asked.

PFEW!

Calix spit a mouthful of cold mash potatoes and chicken breast in Rumor's face. "Bitch, you better kill me...'cuz when I get out this bitch I'ma tear yo' mufuckin' head off ya shoulders. That's on everything I love."

Rumor was not fazed by his threat in the least. "Save ya energy, boo," she told him before covering his mouth with the duct tape. "You'll need it." With that said she stood to her feet and walked towards the door. When she went to close the door behind herself she heard Calix's unnerving muffled cries.

Rumor gradually walked back over and kneeled beside him. Against her better judgment, she pulled the tape off his mouth so he could speak.

"Baby, I'm sorry!" Calix bellowed. Globs of mucus trickled from his nose and ran down his mouth and chin. "I'm so fuckin' sorry. I fucked up!" he cried.

In all her twenty-six years of living, Rumor had never ever seen a grown man cry. Calix looked absolutely pathetic, but she really enjoyed having the power for once. All throughout their seven-year long relationship, she'd allowed Calix to take the driver's seat. He was supposed to be the strength in their unity, but he'd taken her heart and trust and crushed it in the palm of his hand.

"Please! Let me go," Calix pleaded. "You say you a love a nigga, but how the hell can you treat me like this? This shit is crazy. I fucked up, Rumor. Damn, what else you wanna mufucka to say? I'm sorry!"

Tears streamed down Rumor's chocolate cheeks. She could hear her deceased mother telling her "Love is the most beautiful thing to have, hardest thing to earn, and most painful thing to lose."

"I'm sorry too," Rumor said before covering his mouth.

Calix began thrashing about wildly after she walked away. He couldn't take another day being locked away in the garage. It was driving him mentally crazy.

Rumor had lost her sympathy for him a long time ago. He didn't have any for her when he laid down her sister so she refused to have any for him. Ignoring his muffled screams, she turned off the light switch and closed the door behind her.

***

Aso led Jude inside a vast, luxurious office that had a lofty feel to it. White furniture decorated the charming room, and in the corner was a small stage where a busty blonde spun around a bronze pole.

Seated behind a $900 white office desk was King, the mastermind and overseer of the entire car theft operation. The smug expression on his face made him look twice as intimidating. He resembled Compton native rapper, The Game but his face was tatted up like Wayne's.

The atmosphere was a lot more 'chill' inside of his office. The rap music was even mellower than in the chop shop.

"King, this my cousin Jude—the nigga I been tellin' you 'bout."

Jude absentmindedly stepped forward and extended his hand for King to shake.

"Sit down," King said, not bothering to shake Jude's hand.

Jude felt disconcerted and out of place, but nevertheless he remained cool, calm, and collected. He took a seat across from King in a comfy white chair. Aso stood by his side with his hands clasped in front of him. He looked like a parent standing next to his child in the principal's office.

The expansive office began to feel claustrophobic

to Jude. *I can't believe I'm about to step into some shit I ain't got no business being in.* The thought of prison caused discomfort, but Jude remembered that he was doing this shit for his family.

"Aso told me you know a lil' somethin' about cars," King said. His New Orleans accent was strong.

"I used to have my own lil' lot out in Cleveland," Jude told him. "Before that I worked with my big brother at his in Columbus. We been fuckin' with cars for a minute but..." His voice trailed off.

"You ain't never had to steal 'em," King said, finishing his sentence.

Jude shuffled nervously in his seat. His eyes traveled to everything in the room before settling back onto King. "Yeah...exactly..."

King sat back in his seat and gave Jude a side eye. He looked tough but he could tell the young dude was a good guy. He didn't seem as reckless and audacious as the other members. Maybe Jude could prove to be an asset to his business after all. With all of the incoming orders, King could definitely use more niggas to steal the cars.

"Just curious," King began. "What you pushin'?"

"Well I *did* have a 2012 Fisker Karma," Jude answered. "That bitch was clean too...but I told my girl to sell it 'cuz she really needed the paper. I was locked up at the time."

Aso burst out laughing. "Man, you one noble as mufucka," he said. "I would never sell the 'Rati for Lana's ass. I wouldn't give a fuck how broke that bitch was."

King cut his eyes at Aso and he immediately ceased his laughter. Jude's actions were nothing short of being admirable. Respect went a long way with a nigga with like him.

"Aso, I want you to take him out tonight and show him everything he needs to know," King said, looking directly at Jude.

"*Tonight*?!" Jude repeated in skepticism. He'd just made an eleven hour drive to Georgia. He didn't want to do anything but take a hot shower and climb in bed beside his lady.

"Mufucka, did I stutter?" King sneered.

Jude looked down. "Nah, you didn't," he answered. "You were real clear."

"Good. Now get the fuck out my office. Both of ya'll."

6

Justin laid beside Cameron in her plush king size platform bed. Jude should've been lying beside her as well, but whatever he and Aso were doing was obviously more important than spending their first night together in their new home.

Cameron had her head propped on a hand as she scrolled through her iPhone's gallery. There were hundreds of pictures of her, Jude, and Justin during various outings. It seemed ironic when she thought back to the afternoon she nearly aborted her child. Cameron and Jude's relationship started off like a fantasy—until reality finally settled in. Hardships and financial struggles had put a slight burden on their connection...but she hoped this move would correct things.

Musiq Soulchild's *"So beautiful"* played softly on the bedroom's stereo system. Cameron hadn't even started unpacking her clothes, but she made sure the stereo was the first thing she hooked up. The melodies soothed her and kept her mind at ease.

When you're not here...You don't know how much I miss you...

The whole time on my mind...Is how much I'm gonna get to make...

You feel so good...Like you know I could...

Tell me if you feel the same way...

Cameron exited the gallery and went to her contact log. She missed her baby, and she was a little disheartened by the fact that he had yet to call and check on her. She was fighting sleep just to stay awake until he got home.

After locating Jude's name, Cameron went ahead and reached out to him.

***

Jude sat in Aso's passenger seat, and his homeboy Vado sat in the back while they cruised through the busy streets of Atlanta.

When he felt his cellphone vibrate in his jeans pocket, Jude pulled it out and scanned the caller ID. A picture of Cameron wearing a pair of dainty sunglasses flashed across the screen. Her beautiful smile warmed Jude's heart the minute he saw it. Even though the shit he was preparing to do was wrong he felt like it was for the right reasons.

Jude contemplated answering, but he couldn't afford Cameron fucking up his train of thought. He had to be on his toes tonight in order to make a good first impression with King.

Which color should I press, Jude asked himself. *The lime or the red?*

Reluctantly, Jude ignored Cameron's call before replacing his cellphone.

***

Cameron disconnected the call after it sent her to Jude's voicemail. Defeated, she placed her iPhone on the night table, turned the lights off, and climbed in bed with her son. Before sleep engulfed her she wondered if the move to Atlanta was indeed a good one.

***

Hustle Gang's *"Kemosabe"* bumped through the Maserati's audio system as the three men pulled into Onyx's strip club. The rows of flashy cars made the gentlemen club's parking lot look like a showroom.

"I thought we were finna get to business," Jude spoke up. "Why the hell we at a strip club?"

Vado chuckled in the backseat. "Just watch and learn, young nigga."

After parking the car, Aso killed the ignition. An Arabic-looking younger guy ran up to the driver's window. Jude didn't miss Aso slipping the valet employee three crisp hundred dollars underneath a twenty.

"You and Vado gon' 'head," Aso said. "I'ma give ya'll a holla when it's done."

Jude was confused about everything but he decided to go with the flow. He definitely didn't have the money to be tipping hoes so he hoped this was all a part of the plan.

When Jude and Vado made it to the line, they were immediately granted access. Apparently, King had a lot of pull around the city. All of his employees were shown love when it came to nightlife.

Jude followed Vado to the bar where they each took a seat on the barstool.

Vado leaned close to Jude so that he could hear him over the loud rap music. "We gon' have one drink and we each gon' get a lap dance then we rollin' out, aight?"

There was a puzzled expression on Jude's face, but he nodded his head in agreement anyway. "Cool. But what's Aso doin' out there?"

"You seen him pass ole boy them Franks?" he asked Jude.

"Yeah."

"Well, he pretty much paid the dude to slip the Valet ticket off a car's dashboard to make it look like it's parked illegally," Vado explained. "There's a sneaker tow truck parked around the corner."

Jude still looked confused. "But I don't get it," he said. "Why can't Aso just use a Slim Jim or some shit?"

Vado laughed heartily. Apparently, he found amusement in Jude's rhetorical question. "You know how complicated some of these anti-theft systems can be? Nigga, we ain't swipin' no bullshit. We only take high-class cars."

"Can I get you gentlemen anything to drink?" A cute light-skinned bartender asked them.

"Let me get a shot of Patron," Vado ordered.

The bartender turned towards Jude but he appeared to be out of it. He was still absorbing everything occurring around him. It was all happening so fast.

"Sweetie, can I get you anything?" the bartender repeated.

Jude quickly snapped back to reality. "Yeah, lemme get Crown and Coke." He never needed a drink so badly.

**

The following morning, Ericka sat inside her car parked a few houses down from Ms. Patterson's. She was up bright, early, and ready to get into some shit. She hadn't seen or spoken to Jude's mother since his brief stay in the hospital, and she wouldn't be surprised if the feisty older woman hated her guts.

Ericka had his mother's number programmed in her mental contact list. Staring at the quaint, little cottage home she dialed Ms. Patterson's number and waited patiently for an answer.

"Hello?" Ms. Patterson said in a muffled tone. It was 8:30 a.m., and she was still in bed.

"Hey! Good morning, Mama Patterson!" Ericka greeted in a syrupy sweet voice.

Ms. Patterson grimaced on the other end of the line. Waking up to Ericka's voice was the last thing that made a morning good. She would never forget what the young girl did to her son—and with one now deceased— she was twice as protective of her only child.

"What do you want, Ericka?" Ms. Patterson replied smugly. It was way too early for Ericka's nonsense.

Ericka twirled a tendril of curly hair around her slender finger. "You don't sound happy to hear from me, Mama."

Ms. Patterson sat up in bed. "You must think I forgot about the shit you did to my son."

"That's water under the bridge now, Ms. Patterson," Ericka told her. "That's why I'm calling you. I wanted to apologize and make it up to him. I was wondering if you could tell me where he lives. I'd like to surprise him." She was talking to his mother like she hadn't tried to kill him a couple years ago.

There was a brief pause on Ms. Patterson's end, and for a moment Ericka assumed she'd hung up on her. "Hello? Ms. Patterson?"

"Now you listen and listen good, lil' girl. If you touch my son you won't have to worry about the police or going back to jail." The seriousness of Ms. Patterson's tone caused the hairs on the back of Ericka's neck to stand up. "You'll have to deal with me personally and best believe it won't be nothing nice."

Ericka was shocked at hearing Ms. Patterson speak in such a manner. She always seemed so civil and pleasant. Who would've known she had a little thug in her. "Is that a threat?" Ericka asked in disbelief.

"No," Ms. Patterson answered. "It's a promise." *CLICK!*

Ericka pulled her Galaxy S4 away from her ear and stared at it incredulously. For years she wanted nothing more than to be Ms. Patterson's daughter in law...however, after their conversation, Ericka was on the verge of kicking the woman's door in.

"No this bitch didn't," she said to herself. "I should go in there and smack the fuck out her old ass."

Ericka pulled the sun visor down and looked at her reflection in the compact mirror. There was so much anger and hatred in her stormy gray eyes, and it didn't make any sense because she came from a relatively decent home. After smoothing out her wild, curly hair she closed the sun visor.

Ericka's left hand rested on the door handle. She was tempted to get out and give Ms. Patterson a piece of her mind, but she knew that was the wrong way to go about it.

Changing her mind, Ericka switched the gears to drive and pulled off. *Oh, that bitch is gonna get hers. Believe that*, she promised herself.

Ericka's reign of terror had only just begun.

7

"Mornin' bay," Jude kissed Cameron's hair. She sat in a kitchen barstool scrolling down her iPad mini. "What you up to?" he asked, opening the fridge.

Cameron didn't respond as she continued to read through ads.

Jude pulled out a bottle of V8 Splash berry blend and turned to face his woman. "Damn, you ain't talkin' to me now?" he asked.

Cameron finally placed the iPad down and looked up. "I wanted to spend my first night here sleeping beside you," she said. "I didn't even think you would be out all night like that. I even waited up for you."

Jude didn't get in until damn near 5 a.m., and instead of climbing in bed with Cam, he crushed on the sofa. Jude padded over towards her. "My fault babe. I had some business to handle."

"Business like what?" Cameron asked with much attitude.

"*Business*," Jude repeated. He felt she didn't need to know the details.

"Jude, please tell me whatever you're doing is legal."

Jude tilted Cameron's chin up. "What I tell you yesterday? I told you to trust me. Can you do that?"

"Is it legal?" Cameron pressed.

Jude looked her dead in the eyes and lied when he

said, "Yeah, bay. It's legal."

Cameron breathed a sigh of relief. "I hope so, Jude. And don't be lying. I deserve honesty—"

"And you gettin' that," Jude reassured her. "It's legal. I promise."

"Well, how well does it pay?" Cameron asked. "'Cuz these high ceilings are nice and all, but how the hell does your cousin think we can afford the bills here?"

"I'ma take care of all that," Jude said nonchalantly. He started to walk off but Cameron grabbed his arm.

"But this ain't all on you," she told him. "We're in a relationship. That means we both have to play our part. I can get a job too."

"Doing what?" Jude asked.

Cameron hesitated before answering. "I met a girl yesterday who lives a few doors down. She said she dances up at some place called Persuasion," she spoke hastily. "She said she makes great tips—"

"You don't know these mothafuckas out here like that to be tryin' to make friends," Jude said, slightly aggravated. "And you know how I feel about that strippin' shit, Cam. I ain't finna be havin' no niggas droolin' all over my fiancé."

"There's plenty of dancers who have boyfriends—"

"Well, I ain't that nigga," Jude said with finality.

Cameron, however, wouldn't let up on the subject. "I trust you so you should trust me too," she said. "I've never given you a reason to doubt me, Jude."

He gave her the side eye. "So I'm supposed to act like the shit with Silk never happened?"

That was a low blow that Cameron wasn't prepared for. "That doesn't have anything to do with this and you know it. This is about me doing what I gotta do just like you're doing. And let's face it. I make damn good money dancing. We could use that cash—I mean it's nice here and all—but it's nothing like having our own," she said. "It'll only be temporary until we get on our feet and get our own spot. We're a family now...we've gotta build together. I can't just sit back and watch you sacrifice. I'm not that type of chick."

"I know you ain't," Jude agreed. "And that's why I love ya ass..." he paused. "I just feel like...what type of nigga would I be to have you up in these clubs strippin'? You've already been through enough in that type of setting—"

"Well, this isn't Cleveland," Cameron pointed out. "And I'm not as naïve. I'm older now...smarter..."

Jude mulled over the thought. With him working in the car ring and Cameron dancing, they'd definitely make a quick come up. And he damn sure wasn't trying to raise Justin in a home that wasn't his own. "This shit just temporary, aight?"

Cameron smiled. "I would never make it permanent."

"Cool. We agreed," Jude said. "Now what you over here doing?" he asked, looking over her shoulder at the iPad mini.

"I'm on Care.com," Cameron told him. "It's a sight to find trusted nannies. I figured with the both of us working Justin could use the care and attention."

"You trust that?" Jude asked suspiciously.

"They have mom-reviewed caregivers," Cameron assured him. "It's legit. Trust me."

"You find anyone that caught ya interest yet?"

Cameron pointed to a picture of a twenty-six year old white woman with dark auburn hair. Her name was Elyse M. and she had ten years of experience.

Jude's eyes anxiously scanned the provided info. Elyse had First Aid training, she was CPR certified, and even had her own transportation. He frowned the minute he saw her hourly rate. "Ten to fifteen dollars...fuck outta here."

"I'm sure we could negotiate."

"Cool. Call her up then."

***

Cameron ran into Rumor again that afternoon as she was taking empty boxes out. She was letting her dog use the tree for his personal potty and smoking a Newport. Rumor wore a wine colored maxi dress that accentuated every curve on her 5"5 body.

"Miss Cameron!" Rumor called out waving.

Cameron waved back, taking that as an invite to walk over. She was curious about Persuasion.

"It's a beautiful day today, isn't it?" Rumor asked. Her breath reeked of liquor but Cameron wasn't close enough to notice. Rumor woke up drinking and went to bed high. It was the only way she could get through most days after finding out about Calix and her sister.

Cameron shielded the sun with her hand. The hot weather would definitely take some getting used to. "Hot as hell," she laughed.

Rumor giggled. "Girl, you better get you a sun hat or something. This shit's nothin'."

Cameron tried to pretend she didn't see Rumor's dog licking his own crotch. "Just asking, is this a safe area?"

Rumor nodded. "Yeah, it's alright down here. I mean crime is gonna be everywhere but I never had any issues."

"Oh okay...cool," Cameron said. "I don't know why yesterday I thought I heard someone screaming or something. I might've just been tripping though."

Rumor shrugged. "That's weird. I didn't hear anything," she said, knowing damn well it was Calix.

Cameron waved the topic off. "Anyway I was curious about the club you were telling me about yesterday."

"Oh, Persuasion? It's cool. Like I said, I make good money."

"What's a bad night for you?"

Rumor thought about it. "If I'm on my hustle, I'm walkin' out that bitch with at least five hundred."

Cameron nodded her head in approval.

Rumor looked Cameron up and down. "Why?" she

asked. "You thinkin' about coming out of retirement?"

"Maybe..."

A grin tugged at Rumor's full lips. "Well, I'm going in to work tonight. You can ride with me to check it out if you want."

***

"What's up with you, nigga? You over there sittin' quieter than a mufuckin' graveyard," Aso said. He and Jude were riding around looking for a particular vehicle. One of King's clients had put in a special order for a 2012 Mercedes s550.

Vado was in the backseat, talking on his cellphone in Vietnamese. They figured he was talking to his girl or something so they paid him no mind.

"Man, I told Cameron it was cool for her strip," Jude said. "What type of fuck nigga shit is that? Who wants their girl up in a club dancin'?"

Aso chuckled. "Nigga, that's all? Shit, let her get her paper. Hell, that's more income for ya'll. And real talk, cuz, you gotta down ass bitch. Boy, you think Lana would ever lift a finger to help a nigga pay some bills?" He shook his head. "Sometimes I wonder why I even deal with that hoe."

Jude guffawed. "'Cuz you love her ass."

***

"Oh, shit! Fuck me!" Lana moaned. Her perky breasts bounced up and down as she sat in a baseball-catcher position.

Tank pumped ferociously from underneath her. He

used her round, fat ass to guide his strokes.

Lana had told Aso she was going to get a mani and pedi with her girls, but instead of treating her feet and hands, she was treating her pussy to nine inches of thick dick.

"Damn, bitch, you got some good ass pussy," Tank huffed. Beads of sweat rolled off his forehead, and his 8-pack flexed with every stroke he delivered.

Lana reached down and fondled her clit as she bounced up and down on his pole. "I'm about to cum!" she cried out.

"Cum on this dick then," Tank coached her. "Cum on this shit 'til you can't cum no more, baby."

After Lana finally did, she collapsed on top of his rock hard chest. "All this damn sweat," she complained before rolling over.

"What can I say? A nigga put in work."

There was a brief moment of silence between them.

"I really love you, Tank," Lana said breathlessly.

Tank sighed in irritation before climbing out the bed. "I wish you'd quit sayin' that shit." He headed to the bathroom.

Lana quickly climbed out of bed and followed behind. "I can't help how I feel," she argued. "And I really wish you felt the same—"

"I can't do that, Lana—"

"Why not?"

"'Cuz you fuck with my lil' brother!" Tank rounded on her. "Why the hell else?! And besides, you barely even know me for real. You just sayin' that crazy shit 'cuz a nigga make you cum."

Lana stood in the doorway of the bathroom and watched as Tank washed his hands in the sink.

Tank looked a lot like Aso but was a tad bit darker and much more muscular. His hair was cut so low that the next step would have been bald, but it fit his features nicely. His goatee was trimmed neatly and evenly. A mural of tattoos adorned his entire back and upper chest.

"We've been messing with each other for three months," Lana said. "How do I not know you?"

"Just 'cuz I stick my dick in you from time to time don't mean you know me," Tank corrected her. "You really don't know shit about me, ma. Straight up." He had so many dark secrets that skeletons were falling out of his closet.

No one but his brother Aso knew Tank was on the run from the law. Two years ago he had shot Silk in the parking lot of Pandora's Box and left him to die. Those days—and his old stripping job—were behind him now. He kept a low profile for the most part and earned a living as a contract killer. Niggas paid him handsomely to handle their "problems", and he did just that without remorse. Ever since Tank had shot Silk, he knew that he could pull the trigger on another motherfucker if he had to. And for twenty racks he ran up blasting without so much as a second thought.

Work orders were far and few, but Tank continued to save up his paper. He had plans to move out the country and start over.

Lana walked past him towards the shower. "You know I'd leave Aso the minute you tell me you're ready—"

"I'll never be ready," Tank rudely cut her off. "And even if I was I'd never settle for a bitch who'll fuck my brotha. Fuck? You think I'd ever trust a hoe like that?"

Lana ran up to Tank and began throwing weak punches at his back. He quickly turned around and grabbed her little ass up before tossing her onto the rickety motel bed. That type of violent interaction was normal for them.

"Fuck you, nigga!" Lana spat.

Tank climbed on top of her. "Shut the fuck up and open dem legs, bitch."

Lana promptly did as she was told. Their love-hate relationship had her addicted. Tank was like a drug. She knew she shouldn't have been fucking with him, but he made her feel so damn good.

8

Nigga, I ain't worried 'bout nothin'...

Nigga, I ain't worried 'bout nothin'...

Ridin' round with that work, strapped up with that Nina...got to...

Bad bitches with me, molly and Aquafina...

Money don't mean nothing, niggas don't feel you when they see you...

My whole 'hood love me, but na'an nigga wanna touch me...

Persuasion was way more live than any of the strip clubs in Cleveland, and the dancers were ten times as bad. Cameron felt like she was in her old stomping grounds as she followed Rumor through the huge gentlemen's club. There had to have been at least sixty girls on the roster, and there were four dancers on stage at one time. Ordinarily, there was only one dancer at a time when Cameron danced...but she could adjust to a new routine without a problem.

It wasn't even midnight yet and the place was already popping. Some of the baddest women on the planet were employed at Persuasion. Fake tits and silicon-injected asses were on full display like trophy cases. The competition was definitely steep in ATL.

Rumor led the way to the dressing room. "These hoes in here are like fucking carnivores," she whispered to Cameron, looking around at the dancers. "Stay to yourself and make sure to work the floor."

"Girl, you ain't telling me nothing I don't already know. I do this shit," Cameron said confidently.

Her expertise was evident when she emerged from the dressing room twenty minutes later wearing a metallic purple two piece outfit decorated in rhinestones. The baby weight remained in her hips and ass so she looked twice as thick as she did when she first started stripping. A few new tattoos covered her cinnamon skin, and she was by far one of the sexiest females on the roster—even with all the competition.

Instead of tackling the floor head on, Cameron stood outside the dressing room and took in her surroundings. Bills littered the floor, and strippers were tag-teaming the fellas with double dances.

Cameron had promised herself that she was through with the stripper shit, but she'd be lying if she said she didn't feel like she was right at home being there. In a sense it felt like she belonged there.

Rumor appeared alongside her wearing a red cutout one piece and black knee-high stripper heels. "You want one?" she asked, holding out her hand.

Cameron frowned at the two small pills in the center of her palm. "Naw. I'm good."

Rumor casually hunched her shoulders. "More for me," she said before tossing them back. She had to be high in order to perform. Rumor would never be able to be on stage in front of dozens of men half naked while sober. She preferred to dance on the clouds.

"How long you been dancing here?" Cameron asked.

"Four months," Rumor answered. "I was at Pin Ups for a lil' while until they had this big ass shoot out. One of the dancers got killed that night. That shit was crazy."

Hearing the story made Cameron think of X-Rated. That painful evening would forever remain etched in her memory.

"I used to dance up at Magic City but it kinda got whack after a while," Rumor continued. "So I came here...and Persuasion's been treating me good ever since."

Cameron observed her environment. *I'm happy I don't see same the chicks I used to dance with*, she thought to herself. The thought of no one personally knowing her or her past was refreshing. Cleveland was such a small ass city.

"You don't deal with none of these females?" Cameron asked her.

Rumor sucked her teeth. "Look at these hoes. These aren't the type of bitches I'm trying to be acquainted with. They're so got damn clique-ish," she said. "We're gonna form our own clique on these hoes. Watch. Me and you...we're going to be good friends. I can see it." Rumor was confident in a friendship manifesting between her and Cameron. Since she was no longer dealing with her sister and boyfriend the thought of a new friend consoled her. "It's not a coincidence you moved a few houses down from me."

Cameron thought about what she'd just said. She'd tried the whole "friend" thing several times and failed each time miserably.

You don't know these mothafuckas out here like

that to be tryin' to make friends, she could hear Jude saying in the back of her mind.

"We'll see," Cameron said unenthusiastically before walking off.

***

Tank and his partner Axel navigated their way through the busy gentlemen's club in search of an empty table. They finally located one close to the stage. Preparing for some up close and personal action both men took a seat.

Axel and Tank worked together. Standing at 6"6 and weighing a solid 250 lb. Axel was a very intimidating looking man with skin dark as coal. He didn't speak much, and for his profession that was just fine.

An attractive waitress wearing nothing but a black two-piece and mesh stockings placed a tray on their table. An ice bucket contained their bottle of choice. Several bands were stacked neatly on top of each other. They were ready for a long night of unadulterated entertainment.

Now that Tank was no longer shaking his dick for a living it felt good to be the one being entertained.

After popping the cork off their bottle the sexy waitress excused herself but not before collecting a fifty-dollar tip.

As soon as Tank got comfortable his cellphone vibrated twice in his pocket, indicating he had a text message. Pulling out his Droid, he scanned the text's details. He had job to do that involved leaving the state.

Tank's client was paying twenty-five stacks to

have his "issue" taken care of, and that didn't include his flight and travel expenses. After the earnings were split evenly with Axel that left Tank with $12,500. Over ten racks just to put a bullet in a motherfucker's head. If that wasn't easy money Tank didn't know what was.

Tank replaced his cellphone and took a swig from his drink—he nearly choked on the contents after seeing Cameron on stage. He did an automatic double take because he thought his eyes were playing tricks on him.

They don't even see you like I do...First thing when you wake up...

Before you put on your make up...And they don't really know you like I do...

Cause with me you ain't the same...You ain't gotta run no game...

Girl 'cause what you do and what I do ain't different...

We both on a mission...I love your ambition...

Cameron rolled her hips to the mellow beat of August Alsina's "*Get Ya Money*". She looked even better than the last time he'd seen her. *Damn, she thick and fine than a mothafucka*, Tank thought to himself. He licked his thick lips, almost tasting Cameron on his tongue. They'd only had sex one time but the session was one to remember.

At the time Cameron was beefing with her dude Silk. Their conflict had pushed her right into his arms—and ultimately his bed.

Make that money girl it's yours...

Spend that money girl it's yours...

You work hard for all of it, it's yours...

Work that body baby it's yours...

I ain't judging you...

There were two other dancers on stage with Cameron, but she was the only one who had Tank's attention. As a matter of fact, every fella in the club's attention seemed to be on her.

Tank lit an L and watched Cameron put on a performance for the entire club. Several dancers stood off to the side with their arms folded, hating. They were wondering who and where the new girl had just come from.

Tank grabbed two bands off the table and approached the stage. Cameron had just pulled off her top by the time he removed the rubber bands. *Damn, she got her nipples pierced now.* Tank's mouth watered at the sight of her supple breasts. He could still remember the way they felt in his hands and mouth.

'Cause I'm just out here doing what I gotta do...

'Cause all these fuckin bills are due...

And I see all this money to make...So girl you know that I ain't judging you...

Tank tossed a flurry of bills in Cameron's direction. The singles fluttered down all over the stage and floor.

Cameron danced her way over towards the edge of the stage. When she kneeled down in front of Tank she nearly fainted after recognizing his face.

"This must be fate, huh?" he asked with a smile.

Cameron rolled her eyes, stood to her feet, and danced away from him. It seemed like no matter where she went she couldn't get away from her past.

Tank wasn't the least bit offended by her gesture, and for the hell of it, he threw two hundred dollars at her just because. Tank patiently waited for Cameron's performance to end, and when she stepped down he held his hand out for her.

As expected, Cameron ignored his outstretched hand. Tank was like her menstrual cycle. He always popped up unannounced, and his presence was never welcome.

"Damn. You just gon' act stiff with a nigga, huh?" Tank asked.

Cameron tried to act like she didn't even see him. "You know the Feds are looking for you, right?" she asked, not bothering to stop.

Tank grabbed her arm and pulled her towards him. "I ain't worried 'bout that shit. You got all my attention—you always had it," he confessed. "I like ya lil' cut by the way, bay." Tank nodded towards her new hairstyle.

Cameron was a little aggravated by that fact that he liked it and Jude didn't. "Boy, whatever. I gotta go freshen up." She pulled her arm away and headed to the dressing room. She was sure that wouldn't be their last encounter.

Tank chuckled and shook his head as he watched her walk off. Her colossal ass jiggled with each step she took. He loved how she played hard to get. That made the chase even more fun and worthwhile.

Tank joined Axel at their table. Axel had a suspicious look on his face. "You know her?"

Tank watched as Cameron disappeared inside of the dressing room. "I *knew* her," was all he said.

9

Jude's palms were drenched with sweat as he struggled to attach the sneaker tow truck to a silver Mercedes s550. He'd never done anything this intense in life, and on top of that he was doing the shit out in the opening.

To any and everyone else, Jude looked like he was simply towing a car parked at a meter. His dreads were pulled back in a rubber band, and a snapback hung low over his face so that no one could make out his identity. Jude felt like a damn hoodlum as he attached a nylon tow strap to the luxury car.

Aso and Vado sat parked across the street as they waited for Jude to finish the job. "This nigga actin' like stealin' a car is Trigonometry or some shit," Aso said.

Jude wiped the sweat out of his eyes while he struggled to concentrate.

"Hey!" A stocky white guy jogged over towards Jude. "Hey, what the fuck are you doing, man?! This is my car!"

"You parked illegally, man. No parking past eight," Jude lied. "I'm gonna have to take it."

"Like hell you are," the owner of the Mercedes argued. "I ran to the ATM for 5 minutes—"

"And now ya car's gettin' towed. Tough luck, pal." Jude was heartless, but money came before sympathy.

The angry white man stepped to Jude like he was about to hit him. However, Jude didn't give him a chance when he snatched out his 9mm and aimed it at the guy. Seeing the loaded weapon made him stop in his tracks immediately.

"Don't make this shit a murder, man," Jude warned him with a steady aim. "Just back the fuck up off me—"

Evidently, the owner was prepared to die over the fifty thousand dollar vehicle. Without hesitation, he knocked the gun out of Jude's hand and charged him.

Aso and Vado quickly hopped out the Maserati after witnessing the altercation. Instead of running up to help Jude out they wanted to see if he could hold his own first.

Jude's hat flew off his head after he was slammed against the tow truck. He was barely able to recuperate before a fist connected with his jaw.

WHAM!

Aso folded over with laughter as he watched the entire fight unfold. Vado smoked a cigarette while recording it on his cellphone.

It wasn't until Jude tasted blood that he finally saw red. After ducking an oncoming blow, he stole the enraged man directly in his face. Jude could feel the guy's nose break underneath his fist but he didn't stop there. Jude delivered several devastating punches to his chest and mid-section.

"Hit that nigga with somethin' nasty, cuz!" Aso cheered him on.

Jude sent a powerful uppercut to the man's chin that ended it all. The poor guy dropped onto the ground like a puppet after its strings were cut.

Blood looked from the gash on Jude's lower lip, but he didn't feel the pain as he stood over his unconscious victim. His chest heaved up and down slowly. His fists were still clenched tightly, and covered in dark red blood.

"I told yo' ass to back the fuck up off me, nigga!" Jude yelled in anger. He didn't even look like himself at the moment. He looked more like a deranged criminal than a loving fiancé and father. After tonight he would never be the same man.

Aso and Vado sprinted over towards the scene.

"Damn, cuz," Aso said, examining the damage Jude had caused. Thanks to him the guy was now breathing through his mouth instead of his nose. "Come on! Let's hurry up, get this whip, and get the fuck up outta here 'fore somebody call the boys."

***

Hustle Gang's "*G.D.O.D.*" played on maximum inside of the tow truck as Jude cruised along 77. The wind from the lowered window blew through his hair, and he'd never felt more exhilarated.

Jude had been trying to play it safe for so long that he'd forgotten how good it felt to be bad for a change. He felt empowered with another man's blood on his hands. He nodded his head to the erratic beat of the song.

This is what life's all about, Jude said to himself. *Coming out on top.*

***

Cameron sat at the vanity in the dressing room

while she counted her share of the tips. She didn't particularly like that because she was used to keeping all the money. However, sharing a performance with two other dancers had forced to split the earnings evenly.

Suddenly, Rumor appeared in the mirror behind Cameron. Her chocolate breasts hung freely since she'd just finished giving a lap dance. She handed Cameron a glass filled with a clear liquid.

Cameron gave the beverage a funny look. "What is it?" she asked. The last time she'd taken a drink from a stripper it had been laced with ecstasy.

"Chill. It's just Ciroc," Rumor told her.

Cam took the glass from her and tossed it back. She could definitely use a drink. Now that she was finally twenty-one she no longer had to sneak and drink. It seemed like just yesterday Pocahontas had snuck Cameron some Grey Goose disguised as a water bottle.

"There's somebody out there that wants to holla at you," Rumor said.

Cam shook her head. "I'm not stuttin' Tank tonight, period."

Rumor laughed. "Well, I don't know *who* and *what* the fuck a Tank is, but I guarantee this nigga will be *well* worth your time."

Cameron's interest was instantly piqued. After touching up her makeup, she followed Rumor to the VIP area of the club. There were a bunch of fellas dressed in black standing around, drinking, and bopping their heads to the music.

"Excuse me, excuse me," Rumor said wiggling through the guys.

Someone pinched Cameron's ass cheek as she walked past, but it didn't bother her because she knew that came with the territory. When they finally made it through the posse, Cameron saw what all the fuss was about.

O' Zone, an up and coming rapper, sat in a booth across from GGE's CEO and producer, Zeus Carmichael.

Cameron's eyes widened in disbelief; this was her first time ever seeing *real* celebrities. Zeus' $5000 diamond pinky ring glistened in the dimness of the strip club. He was even bigger than he looked on TV, standing at a massive 6"5 and weighing a solid 275 lb.

O' Zone was just as attractive as he was in the videos and magazines. His dreads fell to the middle of his back and the tips were colored a soft light brown. His chestnut skin was covered in body art, and there was a tattoo of a musical note near his right eye.

O' Zone looked fly as hell in a $500 Givenchy shirt, fitted leather pants, and spiked Louboutin sneakers. The jewelry around his neck and wrist sparkled like a light show.

Rumor gave Cameron a gentle shove towards Ozone when she saw her standing there with her mouth agape.

"I saw ya doin' ya thang on stage, shawty. So I had to check you out." O' Zone smiled, revealing a twenty thousand dollar grill. "Why don't you gon' 'head and dance for my patnah. Let me see what 'cha workin' with. If I like what I see I'ma fuck with you, ya dig?"

Cameron looked over at Zeus who seemed more preoccupied with his cellphone than the half-naked women walking around.

"Gon' 'head, girl," Rumor said, nudging Cameron towards Zeus. "Don't be scared. You do this shit, remember?" she teased.

Lil Wayne and The Weeknd's *"I'm Good"* blared throughout the club. Cameron shyly climbed onto Zeus. He was so big, she felt like a small girl climbing into Santa's lap. Zeus looked a little irritated by Cameron's intrusion.

"What's wrong?" she whispered in his ear. His thick beard tickled her skin. "You don't like what you see?" Cameron had perfected the game most dancers spit to the customers. In fact, Pocahontas had taught her everything she knew as far as the hustle went.

Zeus finally paid attention when Cameron began gyrating in his lap. His Clive Christian cologne smelled like heaven. "You know you bad as fuck. You don't need a mufucka to tell you that shit." Zeus' voice was deep and rich.

"Sometimes I need reassurance," Cameron flirted.

Someone from behind made it rain on her as she continued to dance for Zeus. Rumor was preoccupied dancing for the group of fellas standing at VIP entrance. There was so much money surrounding her on the floor that she could pay her rent up for three months.

Zeus smirked. "Don't tempt a nigga like me, shawty."

10

"What happened to your face?" Cameron asked after Jude stumbled into the house around 4 a.m. There was a small cut on his lower lip and a purplish bruise on his right cheek.

When Cameron went to reach for Jude's face he moved her hand away. "It's nothin'. Me and Aso went out drinkin' and ran into some niggas. They ain't want no smoke for real." The strong smell of alcohol seeped from his pores, and judging from his glassy eyes he was also high as a kite.

"We've been in Atlanta for two days and you're already fighting."

Jude brushed past Cameron and walked into their bedroom. "I already gotta mama," he said, pulling his t-shirt over his head. "I don't need another."

Cameron folded her arms and shook her head. "I really hope you don't let this move change you, Jude. Remember what comes first."

Jude waved her off. "I'ma always be the same nigga you met two years ago," he said. "Everything I do I do it for you and my son...you ain't gotta never doubt I'd forget what comes first. I breathe and wake up every day for ya'll, straight up."

Cameron held her hands up in mock surrender. "Alright, Jude. Alright." She climbed into the bed and pulled the sheets over her.

Jude joined her wearing nothing but his Acne jeans.

"Look, I ain't tryin' to bump heads with you." He kissed Cameron's ear, causing her to shiver. "I wanna take you out tomorrow."

Cameron turned over and faced him. "Really? Just me and you? Not me, you, and your cousin Aso?" Her tone was laced with sarcasm.

"Just me and you," Jude confirmed. "And our son, of course." He kissed her forehead, then the tip of her button nose, then her pouty lips. "These last few weeks been hectic and I know shit's been lightweight rocky...but tomorrow I just wanna take the time to remind you why you said to yes a nigga." Jude picked up her left hand and kissed the finger which should've sported an engagement ring. Soon he'd be able to afford the biggest rock he could find.

***

The following morning Rumor stood naked in front of her bathroom mirror. After staring at her own reflection for ten whole minutes, she finally opened the medicine cabinet. There were several bottles of prescription pills lined up on one of the shelves.

Rumor popped a pill from each prescription bottle and slammed the medicine cabinet close. When she looked at her reflection again there were tears in her pretty dark brown eyes. She could feel her body heat rising as emotions overwhelmed her. Thoughts of suicide seemed to come on a regular, but for some reason she had yet to go through with it.

Tears slid down Rumor's cheeks before landing in the bathroom sink. The pain in her heart cut so deep. It was almost unbearable. Sometimes she wondered how and where she got the courage to climb out of bed every day. Rumor could only get through the days if she were either drunk or high. She hated to be sober. When she was sober she thought too much. The drugs and liquor temporarily took her away from a world of pain. Her problems seemed to vanish, and she felt as if she were floating in the sky.

Rumor slowly made her way over towards the claw foot tub and turned on the faucet. A pint of Hennessey sat at the foot of the tub. As warm water filled it, Rumor washed the medication down with dark liquor.

Suddenly, her cellphone began ringing on the bathroom's counter. At first Rumor decided to ignore it as she continued to chug the Hen. The caller was persistent seeing as how they called three more times.

No longer able to ignore it, Rumor stood to her feet. She swayed with each step she took as she made her way over towards her phone. The moment she saw the caller ID she rolled her eyes.

"What do you want?" she sneered.

"I've been calling you like crazy," Roxie said. "We have to talk at some time or another, sis."

Roxie was only twenty years old, and had chosen to grow up incredibly too fast. Following in her older sister's footsteps she was a full time stripper up at Blue Flame. Roxie had tried the whole college thing after barely graduating high school but that style of living obviously wasn't meant for her. She took a different route instead.

"We don't have shit to talk about," Rumor spat.

"Sis, I'm sorry!" Roxie blurted out. "I can't even find the word to express to you how sorry I am. I messed up bad! I was selfish—"

"When are you not selfish?" Rumor cut her off. Roxie was the youngest child so she was spoiled beyond belief. Everything had to go her way, and she had to have everything—including Rumor's man.

"Please, Rumor...this is already hard enough for me—"

"*Hard enough for you*?!" she repeated skeptically. "Bitch, you fucked my fiancé. You're my sister!" Warm tears slipped from Rumor's eyes and cascaded down her face. "I'll never be the fucking same after the shit ya'll did!"

"Rumor, I—"

"I miscarried three days ago!" Rumor yelled.

There was a long pause on Roxie's end after hearing that shocking revelation. "I'm so sorry, Rumor. I—I didn't even you were preg—"

CLICK!

Rumor quickly disconnected the call. The conversation had her blood boiling. No one had even known she was pregnant. She'd even kept that secret from Calix for fear of how he'd react. Nevertheless, Rumor was ecstatic about being a mother even though her doctors had warned her about "possible consequences". Everything was going smoothly up until an oversized blood clot dropped into the toilet while she was urinating. It was exactly two days after she'd found out about Roxie and Calix. Naturally, she blamed them.

The sudden thought of Calix reminded Rumor that she had to feed him. She couldn't have his trifling ass dying on her yet. *Fuck that! His ass has to suffer*, Rumor said to herself.

Tigger skipped alongside her as she quickly made her way into the kitchen. When she opened her refrigerator she noticed that she desperately needed to go grocery shopping. A carton of rotting strawberries sat on the top shelf. After grabbing them, Rumor made her way inside the garage.

Calix was awake and alert that time. Rumor watched as he squirmed around in the darkness.

"Good morning, baby," she greeted before flicking on the light switch.

"*Mmmm*." Calix's muffled screams fell upon deaf ears.

Rumor sauntered towards him and leaned down over him. Aggressively, she snatched the duct tape off his mouth.

"Come on, Rumor. Quit fuckin' around! I gotta take a shit!"

Rumor laughed and shook her head. "That sounds like a personal issue," she said.

"Man, you can't leave a nigga like this," Calix cried. "I'ma die—"

"I'm not gonna let you die," Rumor promised.

Calix looked like a little bitch as he sobbed hysterically. Mucus oozed from his nose and slid over his lips. He wanted to believe his fate's outcome would be a good one, but fucking with Rumor he wasn't so sure.

"You promise?" he asked in a weak voice.

Rumor grabbed a handful of strawberries and forced them in Calix's mouth. The strawberries were so rotten that they were no longer firm. Instead they were soft, soggy, and squishy. They even had a weird smell to them.

"What the f—bitch!" Calix yelled.

Rumor threw the strawberries at him. They bounced off his face and head like ping pong balls. "Did you even wear a condom you trifling motherfucker?!"

"Man, chill!" Calix screamed, trying to duck the flying fruit.

"Did you fuck her raw?!" Rumor hollered.

"Yeah! *Damn*!" Calix answered in defeat.

Rumor struggled to stand to her feet. When she was finally upright she nearly lost her balance. She had to grab a nearby wall to keep from falling.

"Please, Rumor..." Calix begged. "Please let me out of here."

Rumor covered her mouth with a shaky hand. Tears streamed down her cheeks.

"Bitch, lemme outta this shit!" Calix barked. He began thrashing about on the garage floor. "Lemme out! Bitch, I'ma kill you with my mothafuckin' my bare hands! You hear me?! You fuckin' dead!"

Rumor ran over to him and covered his mouth with the duct tape before any of her neighbors could hear him yelling.

11

    That afternoon Jude took Cameron and Justin to the Georgia Aquarium before treating them to lunch in Atlantic Station. Afterward they all did a little shopping at Lennox Mall and Phipps Plaza. Jude brought him and his son matching J's, and Cameron a golden Michael Kors logo watch. When she asked about the money, he lied and told her it was a signing bonus. Jude never gave Cameron a reason to distrust him so she took his word for it.

    King gave Jude eight racks for the Mercedes Benz with intentions on selling it for half its retail price. With the convenient cash flowing in, Jude planned on spoiling the hell out of his girl and son. He was just that type of dude. And since the work was moderately easy, Jude didn't plan on quitting or telling Cam the truth any time soon.

    Cameron, however, was hiding a little secret as well. Last night at Persuasion, she'd given O' Zone her number. Cam loved Jude very much, and she could never see herself stepping out of their relationship, but it wasn't every day one of ATL's hottest upcoming artists asked for her number. Cameron figured if she played her cards right she might be able to get something good out of it. *Keep all "potentials" around*, Pocahontas would say.

    "You should fuck with a nigga," O' Zone told Cameron as he plugged his number in. "This may be a once in a lifetime opportunity."

    Cameron didn't know how true his statement was, but at the moment she had no intentions of finding out. If he wanted her attention he'd have to catch her at the club.

That way he'd have no choice but to spend money.

When Cam and Jude pulled up to their townhome, Aso's Maserati was parked out front. Disappointment washed over Cameron because she felt like Jude was spending entirely too much time with Aso and not enough with her and Justin.

Aso climbed out of his car at the same time Jude and Cameron did. "I was just finna call yo' ass," he said.

"Wassup?" Jude asked him.

Aso nodded towards his car. "Ride with me to drop my brother off at the airport real quick. I gotta holla at you 'bout some shit." He didn't want to say too much while Cameron was around. From the corner of his eye, he peeped her outfit. She wore a cheetah print pencil skirt, peach crop top, and gladiator sandals. The skirt hugged her hips and ass nicely.

"Yo' brother in the car?" Jude asked, walking over towards Aso's Maserati. "Shit, lemme say what's up. Come meet my other cuz, Cam."

Holding Justin's hand, Cameron begrudgingly trudged over to the flashy car. She nearly fainted when she saw Tank's face. An unsettling feeling resonated in the pit of her stomach after realizing Tank and Jude were cousins.

What a small ass world.

A sneaky grin crept across Tank's lips.

***

"You trying to get out? I could use some fresh air," Cameron said as soon as Rumor answered her phone.

"Is everything okay?" Rumor asked. There was concern in her tone.

"It's…Girl, I don't wanna talk about it over the phone. I'd rather vent in person."

Rumor understood. "Alright, give me about a half an hour to get dressed. I'ma come down to your house."

"Cool," Cameron agreed. "I'm about to call my babysitter."

***

"Fuck you over there smilin' for, nigga?" Aso asked, noticing the Kool-Aid grin on Tank's face.

"Oh, nothin'," Tank answered casually. "Nothin' at all." On the low, he was laughing at the fact that he'd fucked both Aso and Jude's girl.

Tank was just as surprised to see Cameron as she was to see him. Aso had told him that their cousin Jude was moving down to Georgia with his girl and kid. However, he would've never guessed Cameron was his girl.

Small fucking world, Tank thought to himself.

Jude sat in the back seat completely oblivious to the fact that both his cousins were digging his girl.

***

"Hey, Rumor this is Elyse. Justin's baby sitter."

Elyse and Rumor shook hands. In Elyse's left arm she carried Justin—who was far too big to be getting carried around. Nonetheless, Jude and Cameron had the toddler spoiled.

An uncomfortable feeling took over Rumor as she looked at Justin. It made her think about the pregnancy...the loss...the pain.

"How are you doing?" Elyse asked.

"I'm fine," Rumor said, not taking her eyes off Justin.

Cameron was too busy grabbing her rolling suitcase and belongings for work that she didn't notice her new friend eyeing her son suspiciously.

"Alright. I'm all ready," Cameron said before kissing Justin on his tiny forehead.

Elyse and Justin stood at the window as they watched Cameron and Rumor disappear inside of Rumor's candy red 2013 Lexus ISC. It was Calix's most prized possession.

Elyse and Justin waved Cameron good bye until she disappeared.

***

After dropping Tank off at Hartsfield-Jackson International Airport, Aso headed to King's warehouse.

"I thought you said you had some shit to holla at me about," Jude said.

"We gotta meetin'," Aso simply said. "I ain't wanna say too much while ya shawty was around, ya dig?"

King's meeting room looked like a Wall Street conference meeting with a long oak table positioned in the middle. Thieves, mechanics, brokers, and even a few police officers sat behind the huge table.

King sat at the head of the table like the father of a household. Aso and Jude quietly took their seats as the meeting unfolded. Once everyone who worked for him was accounted for and present, King stood up from his seat and gradually rounded the table.

You could hear a pin drop. There was so much tension in the room as everyone waited for King to speak.

"...Before we begin—" King snatched out the Glock in his waistband and pointed it in Jude's direction!

POP!

12

Jude and Aso jerked back after the unexpected gunshot, but the bullet wasn't intended for either of them. It struck Aso's partner, Vado directly in the shoulder near his collar bone. Chairs scraped against the linoleum floor. It was obvious that the gunshot had caught everyone off guard.

"*AH, SHIT!*" Vado cried out in pain. His face turned beet red as blood gushed from his wound.

Jude's heart hammered in his chest rapidly. He didn't even see the shit coming, nor did he know why it wasn't happening. *I ain't bargain for all this shit,* Jude said to himself.

King stormed over to Vado and viciously jammed his thumb inside his bullet hole. "Don't shit go down in this mufucka that I don't know about!" he spat.

"*AAAAHHHH!*" Vado screamed in agony.

Enraged for whatever reason, King backed off and pointed to two husky guys sitting on the opposite end of the table. "Strip this, nigga!"

Jude watched in disbelief as the two men tore Vado's clothing off while he continued to bleed profusely. After they stripped his t-shirt off a wire taped to his slender chest was revealed.

Vado was an informant working with the Feds to bring King's entire operation down. During his sporadic foreign phone conversations he was speaking to the law, filling them on any and all information he'd obtained.

The night Vado had recorded Jude's fight on his cellphone was for legal purposes only. Up until now, he'd put on a good front with Aso and everyone else by convincing them that he was one of them.

King had quite a few police officers working for him on the low, and it didn't take much for one to turn over Vado. Never trust sheep was the motto, and it was because of treacherous ass motherfuckers like Vado that made King stand firmly by it.

"Put his ass on the table," King demanded in an eerily calm tone. He swiftly removed his $3500 Hermes belt.

Vado was roughly slammed on top of the long oak table for everyone to see and witness the consequences of being a traitor.

"You made a yaself a target!" King yelled. "You made yaself a target when you did this shit!" *WHAP! WHAP! WHAP! WHAP!*

King's leather belt came down hard on Vado's torso several times, leaving welts after each strike. Everyone watched in silence as he brutally beat Vado worse than a drunken father to his child.

"*AHH! FUCK!*" Vado tried his best to shield the blows, but that didn't stop King from slapping him across the face and stomach with his Hermes belt.

King didn't let up until he saw Vado's flesh tear open. By the time King finished his assault Vado's body was red, bloodied, and riddled with welts and bruises.

Jude sat speechless as he watched Vado groan in

pain. *What the fuck did I just step into?*

King wiped the perspiration off his brow while breathing heavily. "Tie this mufucka up until I figure out what the hell to do with his ass," he said, refastening his belt.

The two guys holding down Vado dragged his bloody and beaten body from the meeting room.

The show, however, was far from being over. King took everyone by surprise when he aimed his Glock at Aso. "You knew about this shit, young nigga?" he asked with fury in his hazel eyes.

Aso instinctively jumped out of his seat and backed up. Holding his hands up defenselessly, he said, "My nigga, on everything, I ain't know that cat was working with the Feds. I put that on my life, man. I'm just as shocked as you!"

King's finger rested on the trigger as he debated whether or not to murk Aso's ass just because of his suspicions.

Jude bravely stood to his feet and stepped in front of Aso. "Man, I know my blood," he boldly said. "He ain't no traitor, bruh."

King licked his dark lips and his nostrils flared wildly. He was tempted to squeeze the trigger anyway, but there was something in Jude's eyes that made him reconsider. There was a humbleness that he had yet to see in any of his other employees.

Slowly, King lowered his gun and turned towards all his workers. "Take notes mufuckas. That's what happens to a nigga who goes against the team!"

***

Cameron and Rumor sat in a booth smoking blueberry flavored hookahs while Cameron informed her on the shocking news. They were at a subtle day club in Midtown enjoying their afternoon before the sun went down, and it was time to make it clap.

"So did you tell him?" Rumor asked.

Cameron took an aggressive pull on the fruity tobacco and blew the smoke through her nostrils. "Girl, hell no! Jude would probably flip if he knew I slept with his cousin. He'd be so hurt and disappointed. What nigga wouldn't be?"

"Well, how long ago was it?" Rumor asked.

"It was over three years ago," Cameron answered honestly. "So long ago I can't even remember if it was good or not."

"Bitch you lyin'," Rumor laughed.

Cameron giggled. "I am. It was great," she admitted. "But it's neither here nor there because I'm with Jude and I will never have eyes for another guy."

"Not even a *certain* rapper," Rumor hinted.

As if on cue, O' Zone texted Cameron's cellphone. The brief message read: *You gon be up at the spot today? I'm tryna get up with you.*

Cameron knew it was a bad idea to give O' Zone her number from the start, but instead of following her best judgment she did the opposite. Cameron replied with a simple 'yes' and O' Zone responded with: *Cool. I'ma see you at the club tonight...and hopefully after too...*

13

That night King, Jude, Aso, and a few other members filed inside of Persuasion Gentlemen's Club. After riding around solely for the pleasure while smoking loud and drinking lean, the gang had somehow ended up at the popular entertainment establishment.

The Sprite and 2 oz. of cough syrup inside his Styrofoam had Jude so messed up that he forgot Cam worked there. The syrup had him feeling like he had tunnel vision. He felt great and without a care in the world. He'd never seriously been into drugs, but he had to admit the temporary high made him feel invincible. Jude's dark reality seemed nonexistent. Vado being viciously beaten to near death with a snakeskin belt seemed insignificant.

Jude felt like he was drifting on clouds as he followed the gang to the VIP section of the strip club. King and his boys looked like the black Goodfellas as they swaggered inside dressed in expensive clothing and custom jewelry.

Cameron was so busy smiling in O' Zone's face that she didn't even notice Jude walk in the club. She and the forthcoming music artist were posted on the wall near the pool table room talking.

"You need to quit bullshittin' and let a nigga take you up out this shit," O' Zone told Cameron said. "If you were my chick ain't no way I'd have you up in here strippin'." He seductively ran a band along her thigh as he leaned in close to her ear. "I'd make you my own personal stripper." O' Zone handed the Cameron the band of cash and she gladly accepted it. He was breaking her off just for the conversation and attention.

Dancers stood off in the distance hating with folded arms because they all wanted the rapper's attention. However, the "new girl" had swept him off his feet with her charming appeal and good looks.

"You ain't like these other bitches. I can tell you different," O' Zone told her. "Right now in my life I need somethin' different..." He pulled Cameron so close that their bodies were pressing together. She could feel his erection leaning against her leg. "Be straight up with me," he said. "Do a nigga really gotta chance?"

"I keep business and pleasure separate," Cameron answered honestly.

"Well, shit...they go hand in hand if you ask me. Especially in this profession," O' Zone added. "We might be able to help each other out." He gave Cameron's round ass a firm squeeze.

Meanwhile, in the VIP room, dancers had flocked to the gang of flashy guys. Everyone but King and Jude were entertaining the strippers, and behaving recklessly with their money. The promethazine codeine and soda had Jude leaning.

King fired up a Cohiba Behike cigar and took a seat next to Jude. "You a real low-key ass mufucka, huh?" he asked, noticing Jude's blasé demeanor. He was the only one in the posse who wasn't hype and throwing money at the half-naked strippers.

"Yeah, I'm pretty chill. Observant if anything else." Jude said. "I've been that way since I was a young nigga. I learn a lot just watchin' mothafuckas and playin' it cool."

King was impressed with the young guy's mature poise. "I can dig it. You learn a lot by just observing shit," he agreed.

The $500 cigar created a thick cloud of smoke in the VIP room. Jeezy blared through the club's entertainment system.

Jude's mind wandered to Vado. "What are you gonna do with Vado?" he asked.

King took a few drags on the cigar as he thought about it. "I'm not sure what I'll do with that mothafucka yet. Without consequences there ain't no lessons to be learned, ya feel me?"

Jude continued to sip his lean as he absorbed King's impressionable words. The last thing he wanted was to end up like Vado, but this lifestyle was definitely proving to be more than what he bargained for. One thing was for certain; he couldn't trust any person with power. If Jude continued to play it safe then hopefully he'd stay on King's good size.

Jude nodded his head to the bass of the music as his dark eyes scanned the dimly lit club. They stopped on Cameron the moment he saw her and O' Zone cozied up together in the far end of the strip club. He had one hand resting on her ass cheek and the other held onto her tiny waist.

Anger resonated in Jude's heart. Jealousy instantly consumed him. He promised Cam that he could deal with her job, but seeing her in action had him seething inside. There was no way in hell he could sit back and watch any longer.

High off promethazine, Jude stood to his feet and left the VIP room. One of the dancers tried to get his attention as he stalked past her, but the last thing on his mind was a lap dance.

Seeing the smile on Cameron's face pissed him off most of all. *Is this why she wanted to start back dancing*, Jude asked himself. *For the attention?*

When Jude reached Cameron, he snatched her out of O' Zone's face by her arm. He was so high that he didn't even recognize the rapper immediately. But even if he did he wouldn't have gave a damn.

"Ow, Jude. You're hurting me," Cameron complained.

Jude didn't ease up on his grip as he led Cameron away from O' Zone and to an empty area in the club. "I said I was cool with this shit but I ain't, Cam. I can't sit back and pretend to be cool with these hard up niggas grabbing all over you. You finna be my wife," he stressed.

"Jude, we already talked about this. This is my job."

Jude gave Cameron a suspicious look. "Be real with me, Cam. You missed this shit. That's all it is. Just admit."

"That's not it at all," Cameron lied.

"You missed this strippin' shit. You missed this lifestyle. You missed the money. You missed the attention—"

"You're drunk and talking crazy," Cameron waved him off.

"I'ma tell you like this," Jude began. "Don't lose a real nigga chasin' after the shit you *think* you want in the streets..." He warned Cameron. Looking over her shoulder he noticed O' Zone watching them intently. There was a look of irritation on the rapper's face. "You got somebody waitin' on you," Jude said before walking away from his girl.

Cameron shook her head in irritation. *The nerve of this nigga to try to tell me about myself.* She was fuming inside but only because the truth hurt. Jude had hit the needle on the head with his statements. Sometimes he knew her better than she knew herself.

After Jude walked off O' Zone walked up to Cameron. Pulling his sunglasses off, he casually asked, "That's yo' nigga or somethin'?"

Cameron grimaced as she watched Jude grab a random dancer by the hand and lead her to the VIP room. *Why the fuck is he even here*, she wondered. "No," Cameron answered dryly. "He's not."

"So look, I'm sayin' tho, shawty, I'm finna dip up outta here 'fore I spend my entire savings account on yo' ass."

Cameron smiled. "That wouldn't be so bad."

O' Zone kissed Cameron on forehead and Jude didn't miss the gesture when he looked back over his shoulder at them.

"For you it ain't," O' Zone said. "Anyway I'll be shootin' a video in a couple weeks and I want you to fuck with it. Bless the screen with ya lovely presence. You think you'll be wit' it?"

"Let me think about that," she told him. Honestly, she had no intentions of going through with it.

O' Zone grabbed Cameron's hands and placed a soft kiss on the back of them. He was trying to finesse her to get her on his team, but unlike most of the chicks he ran into, Cameron was playing hard to get.

"Don't take too long to think about it. Aight, love?"

"Okay."

"I'll get up wit' you later. Best believe, I'ma wear that ass down. When I'm through with you, you ain't gon' wanna deal with nobody else but me, ma," O' Zone promised. He lingered holding onto her hands before he finally walked off.

Envy mixed with the drugs had Jude boiling with rage. Just to be spiteful, he decided to get a little too extra touchy feely during his lap dance. He was hoping that Cameron saw him so that she'd be equally as jealous.

Cameron was walking to the dressing room, thumbing through the band O 'Zone had given her when she stopped in mid-step. She did a double-take when she saw Jude getting a lap dance from a cute brown-skinned stripper. His hands were all over her body as the dancer gyrated in his lap.

Jude looked over at Cameron. The expression on his face said "Yeah, don't feel too good do it?"

Cameron's nostrils flared as she watched Jude grab a handful of the stripper's ass. She'd had never felt so disrespected. *He knows this is my place of business.* Cameron had never known him to behave so petty. In a way, she felt like she didn't recognize Jude. The situation instantly made her think of Silk.

Jude looked back over at Cameron and gave a sneaky smirk. He was acting incredibly immature by purposely trying to make her jealous.

Cameron shook her head while mouthing the words: *Corny as fuck.* Unable to entertain anymore of his childish bullshit, she stomped off to the dressing room.

When Cameron walked inside a few dancers were prepping for their performance. Rumor sat at the vanity, flat ironing her asymmetrical bob. Her glassy eyes indicated that she was already tipsy.

"Hey boo. How's it looking out there?" Rumor asked. "Looking at that money I'm guessing good."

Cameron tossed the band onto the vanity and plopped down in the empty seat beside Rumor. "My life should be a fucking book," she said.

Rumor combed the last little hairs in place, and then applied some edge control to her baby hairs. "You sound like your mind's heavy right now." After replacing the comb inside her oversized purse, Rumor pulled out a small baggie with colorful pills. "Pop one with me and watch the world get smaller."

Cameron stared at the enticing pills with a side eye. Her common sense screamed no, but her lips said, "Alright. Give me one..."

Rumor dropped a miniscule light blue pill in the center of Cameron's outstretched hand. Hoping the drug would make her feel better Cameron placed the pill on her tongue and washed it down with Rumor's shot of Patron.

Rumor failed to tell Cameron that the high would hit her way harder. She was just happy that she wasn't going on her trip alone. Smiling at Cameron in the reflection of the dirty mirror, Rumor tossed back two pills.

In the VIP room, Jude finally got bored with acting like an asshole so he paid his dancer for her services. He dapped up everyone and prepared to leave. Jude was almost at the door when he noticed Cameron climbing up on the stage.

Strange fruit hanging from the poplar trees...

Blood on the leaves...

Cameron grabbed the bronze and did a slow twirl around it. As usual, she had the audience captivated by her unique beauty. Kanye West's *"Blood On The Leaves"* bumped through the club's massive speakers.

The colorful strobe lights reflected off Cameron's soft brown skin. Tiny beads of sweat formed on her forehead and the bridge of her nose. She felt hollow but free at the same time. No one had ever told her that ecstasy felt so great.

Cameron's stomach rolled seductively as she swayed her curvy hips from right to left. Her hands slowly rubbed her flesh in an enticing manner. Bills showered down on her as she performed for the attentive crowd. Cameron's body felt like it was in an orgasmic state.

Before the limelight tore ya...

Before the limelight stole ya...

Remember we were so young...

When I would hold ya...

Before the blood on the leaves...

I know there ain't nothing wrong with me...

Something strange is happening...

Cameron and a fellow light-skinned stripper danced entrancingly on one another. Money exploded onto the stage as a hurricane of bills showered them.

Jude had one hand on the door handle as he watched Cameron. There was something different about her all of a sudden. A part of him wanted to snatch her off the stage and drag her out the club, but then he realized she was there because she wanted to be there. *It was never about us*, Jude concluded. *It was about her wanting to be back in her comfort zone: the strip club.*

Shaking his head in agitation, Jude opened the door and walked out. Cameron was now the one wearing the sneaky grin. Little did she know, this would be the start of a change in the both of them.

***

Cameron sat at the vanity fully dressed as she counted her earnings for the night. Secretly, she really missed the convenient cash. It was all so effortless, and Cameron made it look twice as easy.

"You wanna go to this after party in Decatur with me?" Rumor asked, squeezing her huge ass into a pair of leather shorts.

"I'm tired," Cameron told her. "And my legs are kinda sore 'cuz I haven't danced in a while. I really just wanna go home."

Rumor slipped her feet inside a pair of snakeskin London Trash booties. Cameron had been eyeing those shoes for the longest, but at the time she couldn't afford to buy them.

"Ugh, bitch. You suck," Rumor teased. "And I'm not even going back in the direction of our townhouses."

Cameron waved her off. "It's cool. I'll catch a cab."

"I don't mind taking—"

"No, it's cool. Really," Cameron assured her. "I'll be good."

"Aight then, sexy mama. Hit me up tomorrow. I'm out." Rumor rolled her suitcase out the dressing room, and Cameron stayed behind to call a taxi.

When Cameron exited the dressing room there was a few customers lingering at the bar still even though the stage was emptier than a blank canvas. Dragging her rolling suitcase behind her, Cameron walked outside to get a breath of fresh air. All of a sudden, an arm reached out and grabbed her—

14

Jude pulled Cameron towards him after she stepped outside. She was so busy scrolling through her phone that she didn't notice him standing outside the door.

Initially, Cam was caught off guard but she relaxed a little when she recognized Jude. Pulling away from her baby's father, she brushed past him. "Move, Jude. I ain't in the mood. That shit you did in there was lame as hell." Cameron was so upset with him still that she wasn't sure if she wanted to get in the same car with him.

Jude followed behind her. "I waited until you got off." He was finally coming down from his high, and he could barely remember why he was so upset in the first place.

"Fuck you," Cameron spat.

That feisty shit only turned Jude on. He grabbed Cameron by the elbow and turned her around to face him. He wasn't as aggressive that time, and he used just enough force to let her know he was in control. Before Cameron could pull away from him again, Jude crushed his lips against hers.

At first, Cameron tried to fight the passionate kiss but as soon as Jude slipped his tongue inside she decided to give in. Her anger slowly dissipated as he kissed her in Persuasion's parking lot. From the corner of her eye, Cameron noticed her cab pull up. Seconds later, her cellphone began ringing but she ignored it.

Melting into Jude's body, Cameron closed her eyes and wrapped her arms around Jude's neck. His dreads hung over her shoulders as he pulled her closer. She felt so good in his embrace; so safe and loved.

When they finally pulled apart Cameron noticed that her cab had pulled off but she didn't give a damn. "Don't do any petty shit like that again," she told Jude.

Jude pulled Cameron so close that his erection pressed into her. "You feel that?" he whispered. "I want you like a mothafucka, Cam. I'ma always want you." He suckled her bottom lip and gave it a gentle tug with his teeth. That shit really drove Cameron crazy. "I don't give a damn about these strippers or these bitches in the streets. As long as I got you I got everything. Ya dig?"

The reassurance felt so good to hear. Sometimes Cameron needed it. Grabbing, Jude's hand she led him towards their truck. They couldn't keep their hands off each other for the entire ride home, and Jude had nearly got into a collision after Cameron dropped her head in his lap. Their sensuous session continued all up until they pulled in front of their town home.

Cameron fumbled with the keys as Jude held her from behind and walked with her to the front door. When she stepped on the first stair the house keys accidentally dropped from her fingers.

The keys were the last thing on Jude's mind when he pulled Cameron down onto the stairs with him.

"Boy, what are you doing?" Cameron giggled as she watched him undo his jeans. "Not out here."

"I can't wait anymore," Jude said, lifting her maxi

skirt up and pushing her panties to the side. It was nearly 4 a.m., and there wasn't a single car in sight. The only sound that could be heard was crickets chirping in the distance.

"Baby, we shouldn't—oh, shit," Cameron moaned after he slid inside her. "We shouldn't be out here in the open like this," she said breathlessly. Cameron was saying one thing, but Jude felt so good between her legs.

He nibbled on Cameron's chin as he made love to her on the front stairs of their townhome. "I don't give a damn. Let 'em see our love."

***

The following afternoon, Lana relaxed in the master bathroom's deep garden tub. The thick lavender scented bubbles looked like a cloud of pillows as she reclined in the water. Her iPod nano's ear buds were plugged in and a glass of red wine rested on the edge of the tub.

The tub's jets soothed her body as her fingers stroked her clit underneath the water. Images of Tank pulling her hair and hitting it from behind came to mind. Seconds before she finally made herself cum she felt a hand gently grab her foot. A warm mouth covered her toes, gently sucking on each one. When she opened her eyes and saw Aso her entire fantasy died.

Pulling her foot away, Lana sat up in the tub and removed her headphones. "What are you doing?" she asked, clearly annoyed.

"I saw you in here lookin' like you were havin' a good time and I wanted to get in on that," Aso said.

"I'm not really in the mood for all that right now," Lana said disinterestedly. All she wanted was Tank, but sadly he didn't feel the same. "I really just wanted some solitude. I sucked your dick last night. Damn. Wasn't that enough?"

"Bitch, you ain't never in the mood," Aso complained. "And that's another got damn thing. Everything's about *you*! I swear you one of the most selfish hoes I know. An ole inconsiderate, cocky mothafucka and nobody likes that shit—"

"Oh my goodness. Get out of your fee-fees," Lana waved him off.

Aso stood up from the edge of the tub. He wore nothing but a pair of True Religion jeans. "You know what? I'm startin' to wonder why I even keep yo' black ass around. I'd rather pay for some pussy than put up with the headache you give me—and as a matter of fact I'd be better off just doin' that. It ain't like my bitch wants to fuck me. And then you wanna bring up that weak, half-assed head from last night—you sucked my shit like you barely even wanted to do it. I don't know why the fuck I even bother with ya ass."

Lana plugged back in her ear buds and continued to listen to her Live.Love.ASAP album. Aso's temper tantrum didn't faze her because she knew she wasn't going anywhere.

"Maybe it's about that time I replace ya ass," Aso tossed over his shoulder as he exited the bathroom.

Since the music wasn't turned up very loud, Lana caught the rude comment. "I'm sure Tank won't mind gettin' next," she mumbled under her breath. She'd said it a little louder than she intended to with the music playing in her ears.

Aso was halfway out the bathroom when he turned on his heel. "The fuck you just say?!" he roared.

Lana flinched at the tone of his voice, and one of the ear buds plopped into the bubbly bath water.

"What the fuck did you just say?!" Aso quickly made his way over towards Lana with clenched fists. She shuffled nervously in the tub, but before she could think up a response Aso punched her dead in the nose.

WHAP!

The blow was so unexpected that it sent Lana sinking further inside the bathtub. The warm water quickly turned dark red as blood gushed from her dislocated nose.

"You been fuckin' my brother, bitch?!" Aso yelled. "That's why you been actin' stiff with a nigga lately?" There was so much anger and pain in Aso's voice.

Lana came back up coughing and choking as she tried to suck in air. She couldn't breathe through her nose. Blood gushed down her chin and chest. "What the hell is wrong with you?!" she screamed. "I think you broke my fucking nose!" Lana cradled her injured face as she sat in a tub filled with her own blood.

"Answer the mufuckin' question!" Aso demanded. "Did you fuck my brother or not?!"

Lana held her hands up to protect herself. "Wait a minute. Please, let me explain—"

However, it was too late. Aso grabbed Lana's small shoulders and forced her underneath the water. Her legs thrashed about violently as he held her head beneath the bubbles. Water sloshed onto the bathroom tile but Aso refused to let up.

Lana tried to fight as much as she could but Aso was far stronger.

Reality quickly settled in and Aso realized his actions. "Damn, I'm so sorry baby," he apologized.

Lana coughed and wheezed hysterically as she struggled to breathe. "Get the...fuck away...from me!" she said in between labored breaths.

Aso reached for Lana, but she quickly jumped in fear. The gesture instantly pissed him off because he knew he'd lost her. Without remorse, he snatched a handful of her thousand-dollar weave and forced her back underneath the scarlet bath water.

Lana fought to remain afloat. All of Aso's previous threats had fell on deaf ears. Lana would've never imagined he'd actually hurt her. "Aso, I'm preg—"

Her sentence was immediately cut off when he pushed her head under the red water. Aso didn't release his hold until Lana ceased her kicking and thrashing.

Wiping the perspiration off his forehead, he slowly stood to his feet and looked down at the garden tub.

Lana's body floated lifelessly underneath the rose red water. Her doe shaped eyes were still open and staring at nothing in particular. She'd released her bowels in the midst of struggling.

Without warning, vomit shot up Aso's esophagus, forcing him to rush to the toilet. After reaching it, he lifted the lid and heaved the contents of his breakfast.

Damn. What the fuck did I just do, Aso asked himself.

Wiping the saliva from his mouth and chin, he stumbled into the bedroom where he retrieved his cellphone and called his cousin.

Jude answered on the fourth ring. "What's up? I'm with my lady with right now." He had taken Cameron and Justin to Little Five Points for lunch and sightseeing.

Aso paused and ran a shaky hand over his brush waves. "Cuz, I done fucked up," he said. "I need ya help..."

15

Tank stepped to the side and lit the tip of a Newport with a small lighter.

Armed with a KSG, Axel kicked in the front door of a Raleigh, North Carolina craftsman home. Tank followed him inside carrying a G17 with a silencer at his side.

Mitch Jackson jumped off the sofa after hearing the intrusion. As soon as he saw two men standing in his living room with their weapons drawn he already knew what time it was. Turning on his heel, he ran towards the hallway—

PFEW!

A single bullet pierced his calf muscle.

"*AAHH*!" he cried out, crashing onto the floor.

Tank had perfect aiming since he frequented the shooting range at least several times a week. He kept his Glock aimed at Mitch as he hastily made his way over towards him. He puffed on the cigarette a few times and leaned over the injured man.

"Come on, man! Don't do this shit!" Mitch begged. "I got money! I can pay you! Everything I got is inside a Nike shoebox in my closet. Take it, man! Just don't kill me!"

Tank smashed the lit cigarette into Mitch's cheek.

"*Owwwwww*!" Mitch screamed.

"This ain't about no mothafuckin' money you know it," Tank said calmly. "The nigga King sent me to send you a message." He stood to his feet and aimed the G17 at Mitch's head. "He told me to tell you if want out The Ring then there's only one way to leave."

POP! POP!

Tank put two bullets in Mitch's dome—per King's request.

King had sent Tank after Mitch simply because he wanted to get out of the car theft business. At the moment King seemed understanding, so Mitch took that as the go head to move to North Carolina in hopes of starting over. Unfortunately, King couldn't risk Mitch holding onto the all the information he knew while no longer being an asset to his business. Sadly, Aso had failed to tell Jude that when you worked for King you were pretty much selling your soul to devil. Once you were in there was no getting out.

All of a sudden, Tank's cellphone began ringing. He was surprised to see his brother's name flashing across the screen. "Man, what this mothafucka want?" he asked himself before answering. "Yo?"

"You been fuckin' Lana, nigga?"

Tank sighed in irritation. Now wasn't the time or the place for the petty shit. Nevertheless, he decided to be real with his little brother. "Yeah...I smashed a few times..."

Aso chuckled on the opposite end. He didn't expect for Tank to be so straightforward. "Damn, nigga. You lightweight foul. All the shit I did for you—I put ya ass on to King—it's because of me you even got that mufuckin' job!" he pointed out. "And you been hittin' my girl?"

"Bruh, we gon' have to chop it when I get back," Tank said nonchalantly. "Ain't really the time for this shit—"

"Oh, I'ma see you when you get back, nigga. You can believe that shit." CLICK!

Tank was confused by Aso's statement, but he couldn't afford to entertain him at the moment.

Opening up the camera in his iPhone, he snapped two photos of Mitch before sending them to King's number. Minutes later, the funds were transferred into his bank account.

***

Aso hung up on Tank the minute he heard knocking at his front door. At first, his heart sunk into the pit of his stomach because he feared it was the police. Then he remembered that he'd called Jude.

Aso hurriedly answered the front door and Jude trudged inside. "What's up, mothafucka? You look like shit too by the way," Jude said.

"Nigga, I fucked up!" Aso blurted out. "I fucked up bad, cuz!" He was beginning to panic at the thought of being arrested.

Jude gave Aso a skeptical look. "How bad?" he asked.

Aso led Jude inside the master bathroom. The soles of his Prada sneakers slid on the wet tile. He had to grab onto the wall just to keep from falling. Jude couldn't believe his eyes when he saw Lana's lifeless body resting at the bottom of the tub.

He looked over at Aso in shock and disbelief. "You did this shit?!"

Tears formed in Aso's hazel eyes. "Man, I overreacted!" he ran his bloodstained hands over his hair. "I wasn't fuckin' thinkin', cuz!"

Jude backed out the bathroom. "This ain't got nothin' to do with me. I don't want shit to do with this," he said, walking off.

Aso quickly ran around Jude and thwarted his path. "You gotta help a nigga, fam!" he begged. "I ain't built for no mufuckin' prison life!" Tears slid down his light brown cheeks. "That shit'll break me bruh," he said. "Come on, I came through with the job and the crib. I looked out for you! Look out for me, blood! I can't go to prison!"

Jude's jaw muscle tensed as he thought about what his cousin was asking from him. Sometimes he had too big of a heart.

Aso was his family, and he didn't want to lose another person close to him. Jerrell was already enough. And Jude hated to agree, but Aso definitely wasn't built for the prison life. Emotionally, he was too weak. Physically, he couldn't have been any bigger than rapper, Wiz Khalifa.

Ignoring his better judgment, Jude said, "Damn nigga...you really puttin' me in a hard place right now. Fuck it. You got any gloves, man?"

***

Rumor held a forkful of chicken flavored Ramen noodles near Calix's cracked, dry lips. "Here you go, baby," she said after blowing on the noodles a few times.

Calix looked irritated as he stared at the garage ceiling. "Bitch, get that shit away from me," he cursed.

Rumor giggled. "What's wrong? You not used to eat the broke man's food?"

Calix's nostrils flared in anger. "How long are you fuckin' going to keep me in here, Rumor? Shit, people gon' start askin' questions. You know how many mufuckas I deal with on a regular basis? People gon' start gettin' worried."

"You're going to starve to death if you don't eat," Rumor said, bringing the fork back to his mouth.

Calix turned his head away. "Fuck you, crazy ass bitch."

Rumor's cellphone unexpectedly began vibrating beside her. When she looked at the caller ID she rolled her eyes. Her sister had the worse timing. Placing the bowl of Ramen noodles on the floor ground beside her Rumor answered the phone.

"What the hell do you want? Why do you keep calling me, Roxie?" she asked annoyed.

"I want to talk to you," Roxie cried. "I miss my sister! We shouldn't be letting something like this drive us apart. We need to talk so we can get past this, Rumor. We're all each other got."

"SOMEBODY FUCKING HELP—"

Rumor quickly covered Calix's mouth with her hand.

"Sis?" Roxie called out. "Sis, what was that?"

"It was noth—*Aaahh!*" she yelped in pain after Calix bit her hand. His pearly white teeth tore into her flesh, causing severe pain.

Rumor grabbed the fork off the ground and viciously stabbed Calix in the shoulder.

He instantly released her hand and howled in pain.

"Hello?!" Roxie yelled. "Rumor, say something! What's going on over there? I'm coming over!"

Rumor quickly put the phone back to hear. "No! Don't come over!" But it was too late. Roxie had already disconnected the call.

"I can't fucking believe you stabbed me!" Calix said in disbelief. He looked down at the fork protruding from his shoulder. Blood trickled down his arm.

Rumor hastily covered Calix's mouth with duct tape. If the police weren't already on their way, Roxie sure was. *Why won't this hoe just leave me alone? Sleeping with my man wasn't enough for her?*

Holding her injured, bleeding hand, she made her way to the bathroom sink and ran cold water over the bite wounds. *"Shit!"* Rumor hissed. Her right hand trembled in agony as she tried her best to clean the laceration. "I can't believe this motherfucker bit me."

Tigger ran inside the bathroom and began yapping at her feet since he needed to pee.

Rumor opened the medicine cabinet and pulled out the bottle of rubbing alcohol. Tigger's incessant whining was beginning to get on her nerves. After unscrewing the cap she poured the alcohol over her wounded hand.

Rumor gritted her teeth to keep from screaming. "Fuck me!" she cried out.

Tigger's whines suddenly turned into loud barks.

"Would you shut the hell up?!" Rumor screamed before kicking the shit out Tigger.

He yelped in pain before his little, fragile body slammed into a nearby wall. Whimpering in fear, Tigger quickly scurried out the bathroom before Rumor could cause more harm.

Rumor gasped in shock after realizing what she'd done. Just then the doorbell rang.

"Shit! Shit! Shit!" Rumor cursed. She had forgotten that her sister stayed on 14th street in the Windsor at Midtown. Depending on traffic, it took about five minutes to get to her house.

Rumor opened the medicine cabinet, and hurriedly bandaged her swollen hand. Her doorbell continued to ring reminding her that she also had another issue at the front door.

Quickly making her way to the door, she peered through the peephole. Roxie stood on the opposite side with a worrisome expression on her pretty, youthful face. She was a shade or two lighter than Rumor but was equally as attractive as her older sister.

"Go away," Rumor yelled through the door.

"Come on. Open the door. It's hot as hell out here," Roxie said. "I'm worried about you. And we really need to talk."

"No, bitch, you need to get your ass off my property. I don't have anything to say to you. Not now. Not ever. Now beat it."

Roxie shook her head. "You think handling problems your way are going to solve things when they won't. It'll only make shit worse. You really need to grow up." She turned around and walked back to her car.

***

Rumor waited at the front door for Cameron to grab her things. They were going to the mall and afterward to get a couple drinks. Although Jude had advised her against making friends it felt good to have a girlfriend in a new city where she knew no one. In Cameron's opinion Rumor seemed sane enough and that was all that mattered to her.

After grabbing her green Chanel clutch from the counter, Cameron kissed Justin on his forehead and waved goodbye to Elyse. Now that she'd gotten a little friend she had been dumping her motherly duties on the nanny. Elyse, however, didn't mind the responsibility.

When Cameron climbed inside Rumor's 2013 Lexus ISC, she noticed Rumor's bandaged hand. "What happened?" she asked.

"I...uh...burnt myself earlier," Rumor lied. "Anyway we ain't goin' to the mall," she casually said.

Cameron fastened her seat belt. "What are you talking about? What else did you have in mind?"

Rumor put the gears into drive and smiled.

Thirty minutes later they pulled into the driveway of a beautiful half-million dollar in Alpharetta, Geogia. Rumor parked behind a red and black Bugatti and killed the engine.

"Who lives here?" Cameron asked.

Rumor unfastened her seatbelt and turned towards her. "Don't be mad, but O' Zone has been hounding me and a bunch of other girls at Persuasion about you, Cam. He knew the only way you'd really give him the time of day was if I brought you to him." She left out the fact that he'd also tossed her two racks to do it.

"O' Zone lives here?" Cameron asked.

"No, this is Zeus' home. O' Zone's in the studio," Rumor explained. "He really wants to see you, Cam..."

Cameron looked at the six-bedroom, four-bathroom executive home. "Why'd you bring me here? Rumor, I—I can't be here. My dude would flip!"

"Mind my manners but fuck your dude. Bitch, this is Greek Gang's own O' Zone. You know how many chicks would love the opportunity he's given you."

***

Calix Ramirez reeked of urine, rotting food, and foul body odor. He'd been trapped inside the garage nearly a week. Calix was so famished that it felt like his stomach was touching his back. Rumor was doing a nigga so cold. Sometimes at night he often prayed she'd just go ahead and finish him off. She was fucking with his sanity and that was far worse than a bullet to his head.

I swear when I get out of here I'ma choke this bitch

until her eyes pop out of her damn sockets, Calix promised himself. He would've never thought Rumor would go to these extents to make him suffer. She seemed perfectly normal all throughout their seven year relationship. Who would've known that an infidelity would have been the thing to make her snap?

Mosquitos nibbled on his flesh, and he felt like a carcass that was still somehow breathing life. If he didn't escape, he would surely die at the hands of his girl. There was no limit to the things a woman with a scorned heart would do.

From the corner of his eye, Calix noticed the sharp edge of a broken container lying several feet away. Freedom was imminent after all.

***

Jude drove in silence on the way back home. He would never be the same after that day. Sleep would never come peacefully knowing the shit he'd taken part of with Aso. Georgia was turning Jude into something that he wasn't.

The stench of blood remained in Jude's nose. He could still feel Lana's warm body in his arms as he lifted and dropped her body inside an empty alley's dumpster. The plan was to make it look like she'd been beaten, raped, and left for dead.

Jude ran a hand through his dreads. He was getting himself into way more than what he'd bargained for. Seeing Lana like that made him want to love and cherish Cam more than he already did.

I don't know what the fuck I'd do if I didn't have that

girl, Jude thought to himself. His life would be hollow.

Taking the next exit, Jude made a quick detour. He had to do something to show Cameron how much he cared and how much she meant to him. He also needed something to get his mind off the unspeakable act he'd just committed.

16

"No! Please don't!" Cameron begged.

O' Zone ignored her pointless pleas as he carried her over his shoulder.

"Put me down!" Cameron demanded. "I said put me—"

PSSHHH!

O' Zone finally granted Cameron's wish when he tossed her inside the pool's crystal blue water. Rumor leaped inside the pool seconds after.

Cameron, Rumor, O' Zone, and a few of his homies were lounging on the W's rooftop patio. Ozone had rented out the patio to entertain his crew and new love interest. Bottles of liquor—both light and dark—lined the edge of the pool. Everyone, including Cameron, was high on weed and pills. Jude was always out, not paying her much attention because he was focusing on other shit, and that only pushed Cam closer to Rumor and the party life. She was even beginning to spend less time with her son.

Just because he could, O' Zone threw a handful of money into the pool. His $3700 Givenchy jeans hung low on his waist, he was shirtless, and a solid gold diamond chain hung around his neck. Dangling on the chain was a sparkling pendant in the shape of Africa.

One of O' Zone's homeboys recorded the show on his cellphone so that he could post it to the rapper's Instagram and YouTube account later.

"This how we mufuckin' do it out here in the A,

shawty! We turn up to the sun rise, nigga! Who fuckin' with Greek Gang ENT? Not a na'an nigga! Get wit' it or get run the fuck over!"

O' Zone swaggered over to the pool carrying a small silver tray. On top of it was a white powdery substance.

Rumor waded over towards him to get in on the drug. "You gon' do a line with me?" she called out over her shoulder.

"Nah, I'm good," Cameron declined. She was still feeling herself from the pill she'd taken earlier. "Í should probably be getting ready to leave soon too. I gotta get back to my son. I promised my baby sitter I'd be back by seven."

Rumor sucked her teeth and waved Cam off. "Girl, that lil' nigga straight. You and I both know he's in good hands. Now chill."

"Come on now, shawty." O' Zone said. "We all takin' a trip to the sky tonight. Don't be the only one to get left behind."

Cameron gave the drug a suspicious look. "What is it?" she asked.

"Adderall."

Rumor sniffed aggressively and wiped away her nostrils. "This shit right here...it feels like fucking heaven, Cam."

***

Jude called Cameron's phone for the fourth time that evening. It seemed out of the ordinary for her to be away from home for so many hours, and not answer her phone. It was even worse that she had yet to call and check on her son.

Jude sat with a look of irritation at the dining room table. The table was set up similar to a scene in a romance movie. Two candles sat opposite of each other on the dining room table, illuminating the dimly lit room.

Jude's lone shadow danced against the wall as he wondered where the hell his girl was. He'd planned the perfect evening. After sending Elyse on her way, Jude had put his son to bed, and cooked dinner. Butter poached lobster with tarragon and champagne.

White and red rose petals sprinkled the hardwood floors from the front door to the master bedroom. Sitting in the center of their king sized platform bed was a Christian Louboutin shoebox.

Jude downed the Champagne and stared at his cellphone's screen. He figured maybe if he stared at his long enough his fiancé would call. Cameron had already agreed earlier that she wasn't going to work that night so he didn't know where else she could be.

Jude wasn't the insecure type but he still felt that Cameron could've at least told him where she was going to be. Fed up with waiting on a call/text that was never going to come, Jude stood to his feet and dumped the expensive food inside of kitchen's trash can.

"Fuck it..."

***

O' Zone and Cameron shared a comfortable blue pool side chair as they rotated a tightly rolled blunt.

"I wanna take you out tomorrow and buy you a car just 'cuz...," O' Zone said. His eyes were low and glassy.

Cameron laughed and took the L from him. She hadn't started smoking until recently, and she was only doing to fit in. Jude wouldn't be all too pleased if he knew since he always complained that women who smoked were a turn off. Speaking of Jude Cam didn't even notice her phone ringing on the table beside her. The sound of loud music had drowned out her ringtone.

"You can't buy with me material," she said. Truth be told, she was actually starting to dig him on the low. The promise to keep it professional had gone completely out the window.

"Well, shit...money can buy happiness. What bitch doesn't want that?"

"Not every *woman's* happiness comes solely from materialistic things. Sometimes we want something simpler."

"Like what?" O' Zone asked, pulling on the blunt.

Cameron shrugged. "I don't know. Like getting attention. To feel like we're special. To feel like we come first." She thought about Jude.

O' Zone blew smoke through his nostrils. "You fuck with me and you'll get all that and then some, baby girl."

***

Cameron and Rumor rode back to Midtown with the top down. "Diced Pineapples" played on low. The wind blew through their hair as they enjoyed the peaceful ride.

"You're the only person I'm telling this to—and I

don't even know why I'm telling you...but I guess I gotta tell someone," Rumor said. "I just found out that my sister slept with my man."

Cameron looked over at Rumor and pulled her sunglasses off. "Are you serious?" she asked in shock.

"Dead ass," Rumor nodded her head. "And the bitch has the nerve to be calling me trying to apologize and shit like I want anything to do with her." Since she was drunk and her emotions were all over the place, Rumor was grateful just to have someone to vent to.

"I'm sorry to hear that," Cameron said sincerely.

Rumor chuckled. "Don't feel sorry for me," she said. "Feel sorry for my sister...'cuz even though she fucked my man she really fucked herself in the end."

Cameron was confused. "What do you mean?"

Rumor didn't respond immediately. Cameron was the first and only person she was telling this to. Even though she hadn't known for a while she felt like she could open up and be honest with someone. "Me and my boyfriend, Calix are both HIV positive..."

***

Rumor stumbled inside her townhouse at four-something in the morning. She held her six inch heels in her hand because her feet were too sore to wear them. Tonight's fun had made her forget all about her problems, and the fact that her boyfriend was tied up in the garage.

Most of the lights were off inside. Rumor heard the pity-pat of Tigger's paws before she even saw him. She instantly noticed something dangling from his mouth as he ran up to her. Evidently, he'd forgiven her about the whole bathroom ordeal.

"Boy...what the hell you got in your mouth?" Rumor dropped her bag and keys on the foyer accent table and picked up Tigger. When she finally saw what was clenched between his teeth she could've passed out.

Cable wire.

"I ain't think you would ever come home," Calix said in a low tone. He emerged from the shadows. After hours of rubbing the cable wire against a sharp edge he had finally freed himself.

Rumor accidentally dropped Tigger on the floor. He quickly scurried away yelping.

Calix's fists were clenched tightly as he approached her. There were small cuts and nicks on his hands and arms from trying to free himself.

"Calix...I—how did you—"

"Bitch, I been waitin' all night to get at you! You thought you was just gon' lock me away and not pay for this shit?!" He couldn't figure out if he wanted to beat her to death or strangle her for the shit she'd put him through.

When he finally reached Rumor, he wrapped his large hands around her throat and slammed her against the wall. The back of Rumor's head slammed against the wall so hard that she could've sworn she felt her brain shake.

Calix bared his teeth like a madman as he choked the life out of his girlfriend. "You thought you was gone kill me bitch?!" he yelled. Spit splattered Rumor's face as he hollered. "*Huh*?! Is that what the fuck you thought you was gon' do?"

Rumor grabbed his wrists and tried to pry Calix off but he was far stronger. She hacked and gasped for air as his hands tightened around her windpipe. Her toes were barely touching the hardwood floors.

Without warning, Rumor pressed her thumbs into his eyes, causing him to loosen his hold. She then delivered a swift kick to his left shin.

"Shit," Calix kneeled over in pain. He was the very one who'd paid for her weekly self-defense classes.

"If a nigga tries you and I ain't there to protect you, you gotta know how to defend yaself, babe."

Calix never thought he'd be the one facing her self-defense attacks.

Not giving him a second to recuperate, Rumor grabbed the small ceramic vase off the table nearby, and slammed it into Calix's temple.

He dropped down onto the cherry hardwood floors instantly. The blow had knocked him unconscious for a few moments which brought Rumor just enough time to drag him back to the garage. When Calix finally came back to he noticed he was right back inside of his chamber.

"Crazy...bitch," Calix mumbled. His brain told him to get up and whup her ass, but the strike to the head had weakened him greatly. He felt a step away from being paralyzed. His eyelids fluttered as he stared up at ceiling. "I swear...I'ma end ya existence..."

Rumor ignored his useless threats as she re-tied

his wrists, and legs together with cable wire and duct tape. "Now let's see ya ass get out of that shit," she said cockily. "And you know what? You gotta lot of nerve for being pissed at me. You can't say you didn't see this shit coming? I mean, I can only put up with so much," she vented. "Hell, I pretty much signed my death certificate after finding out you gave me HIV…but yet and still I chose to stay because I thought we could get through this together." She shook her head in disgust. "But then you go and stick your sick dick in my little sister. How could you do that to me?"

Calix's chest heaved up and down slowly. "Please, Rumor," he begged. "I'm sorry."

"Fuck you," she said heartlessly. She then stood to her feet and walked out the room.

Emotionally and physically weakened, all he could think to say was, "I'ma fuckin' kill you…" However, his threat went unheard as Rumor slammed the door shut behind her.

***

Cameron emerged from the master bathroom wearing one of Jude's oversized t-shirts. Although she had brushed her teeth and gargled with mouthwash you could still smell the scent of liquor on her breath. Cameron had taken a risk tonight by hanging out with O' Zone and his crew and guiltily she'd enjoyed herself. Nothing had went down between her and the music artist but if she didn't stop it before it began then something would surely pop off. Something she wouldn't be able to take back.

Climbing into the comfy king sized bed Cameron wrapped her around Jude, and snuggled closely behind him. His dreads smelled so good, and his body was firm yet warm.

Jude stirred softly before grabbing Cameron's arm and pulling her closer. In the beginning, he had intentions to go in on her the minute she walked through the front door, but having her there beside him was more than anything he could ask for.

17

  Jude was sitting at the kitchen island counter, eating a bowl of cereal when Cameron sauntered inside the following morning. Justin sat in the middle of the living room floor, playing Topples without a care in the world.

  When Cameron walked past him he lifted his arms to be picked up but she completely ignored her. Lately, she'd been neglecting him more than usual, and Jude wasn't any better since he worked most of the time.

  Jude studied Cameron's profile for a couple minutes before he said anything. Her beauty was subtle yet she was the baddest chick he knew. He had never put as much trust into a female as he did with Cam, and he hoped like hell that she wouldn't make him regret it.

  "I waited up for you last night," Jude said smugly. He was beginning to notice a slight change in her attitude and body language.

  "I stayed out late last night with Rumor," Cameron answered nonchalantly, not even looking in his direction.

  "Rumor this? Rumor that? You spendin' a lot of time with this chick and you don't even really know her. She could be crazy for all yo' ass knows."

  Cameron looked over her shoulder at him and smirked. "Someone sounds jealous."

  "I was looking to spend some time with you last night and you out runnin' the streets with some broad—"

  "So you can run the streets with Aso and 'em, but

I can't do me. Come on now. Don't be a fucking hypocrite—
"

"I work," Jude corrected her. "What I'm doing, this is for us, Cam. I don't enjoy this shit." And he meant every word of that. His ideal job didn't involve stealing cars for a living. She had no idea all he was doing to provide. He was sacrificing his freedom and putting his life on the line for a few measly stacks. "It's all about business," Jude continued. "Don't ever confuse the two."

"Well, you sure looked like you were enjoying yourself at my job," Cameron retorted.

"That shit's irrelevant. Don't hold it over me," Jude said. "And quit callin' that shit ya job. It ain't ya damn job. It's some temporary—nah, you know what? As a matter of fact, I don't even want you fuckin' with that scene no more. I'm tired of smellin' those niggas on you every time you come home."

Cameron propped a hand on her hip. "Jude is this about me dancing or is this about Rumor?" she asked.

"It's about us," Jude answered. "Cam, these last few days I've been feelin' like I'm startin' to lose you. I don't want this shit to tear us apart. Makin' some quick cash ain't worth jeopardizin' our relationship, on everything, Cam."

"I don't know why you feel like you're losing me. The only reason I started back dancing was to help bring in a lil' more income—"

"And you did that," Jude told her. "And I appreciated it—still do. But now lemme take care us. That's what a man's supposed to do. I got us...I just need to know if you got me..."

Cameron padded over towards Jude, and joined him at the kitchen island. Leaning her head on his shoulder, she said, "I'ma always have your back and you know that. You don't ever have to doubt that."

Jude smiled. "Word?"

Cameron giggled. "You know I'm gonna always remember the very first time we met," she said. "You were all on your cellphone—acting like I was invisible...I had to let you know what was up. You remember that night?"

Jude chuckled and shook his head. "How can I not?" he asked. "You were one of the hottest commodities up in that joint." He tugged on Cameron's shirt and pulled her between his legs. "When you gave me that dance...I just knew I had to have ya ass."

As soon as Cameron leaned in for a kiss there intimate moment was interrupted by the sound of Jude's cellphone ringing.

Cameron grimaced as she handed Jude his cellphone off the counter. He then dipped off into the hallway to answer it. "Yo?"

"Aye, man. King wanna holla at us," Aso said. "Be ready, I'm finna swing by ya crib."

An hour later, King and Aso pulled up to The Warehouse and met King as instructed. Jude was under the impression that he was just going to give them a couple work orders. He was not at all prepared when King led them into an empty room with Vado tied to a chair.

"Dawg—nah, man," Aso turned on his heel to

walk out. He didn't want anything to do with the situation, but King gave him a firm shove.

Jude expected Vado to be dead by now. He would've never expected for King to keep him alive after all this time. Vado looked horrible. His face had been pummeled to the point where he was barely recognizable.

"You're new to the circle so I don't expect for you to know what the hell goin' on," King explained to Jude. "But I have a particular way I like to deal with mufuckas who go against The Ring."

"Man, this was my homeboy at one time," Aso argued. "I ain't tryin' to do this shit, man."

King pulled out his KAP-40 and aimed it at Aso. Jude backed up as well. He barely knew what the hell was going on.

"You gon' do whatever the fuck I tell you to do, lil' nigga!" King snarled. "You work for me! Not the other way around!"

Jude watched in silence as King pulled out a switchblade and cut Vado loose. He then kicked over the chair, causing Vado to fall to the ground. "Handle this crooked ass mufucka," King ordered Aso.

Aso hesitated. Although, Vado turned out to be a traitor they were still cool once upon a time. Reluctantly, Aso delivered a weak kick to Vado's ribs.

The blow was still strong enough to make Vado cry out in pain and cradle his stomach.

King pointed his gun at Aso. "I said handle this mufucka!" he barked. "You wanna be down with my team, well then you gotta prove you can handle the tasks I give you, playa. 'Cuz if you can't, I can lay you down right next to this pussy ass nigga."

Not wanting to end up like his boy, Aso heartlessly stomped Vado a few times, and nearly tripping in the process. He then backed away and threw up his lunch on the cold concrete floor.

King shook his head in disgust. "Fuckin' soft ass nigga. Get the fuck outta here and clean yo' self up."

Aso wiped the drool off his mouth and stumbled out the room. Jude was just about to follow behind him when King pointed his gun at him. "Nah. Not you, pretty boy," he said. "It's 'bout that time you established ya loyalty to the crew." He nodded his head at Vado who was lying pathetically on the floor grunting in agony.

Jude held his hands up defenselessly. "Bruh, this ain't got shit to do with me."

King scoffed and shook his head. "Bitchassness must run in ya'll mufuckin' family," he said. "Either you whup this nigga's ass or you can find yaself another hustle." Of course, King was talking shit. If Jude proved to be unworthy of his team then he would kill his ass without so much as a second thought. King needed niggas on his team that was down to do die for the principal. Weakness was not an option.

Taking a deep breath, Jude swallowed his pride. He didn't really know the dude Vado, but if he had to prove his allegiance to King by whooping his ass then that's what he'd do.

"My bad about this shit," Jude told Vado.

He then proceeded to kick and stomp Vado on the floor like he was being jumped into a gang. When Jude finally tired himself from doing that, he climbed on top of him, and began delivering punch after punch.

By the time Jude finished his assault his knuckles were raw and bloodied. For a second, he thought he might've even killed Vado until he noticed his chest moving up and down slowly. He was alive...but barely.

A slow smile spread across King's thick lips. He was overly pleased with the show Jude had put on.

18

"What you doing, slut? You coming to work tonight?" Rumor asked.

Cameron cradled the cellphone between her shoulder and ear as she sautéed meat for the Chicken Cacciatore. She still couldn't get over Rumor having HIV, but she had no reason to treat her any different.

"Girl, I doubt it. My dude pulled the plug on that dancing shit today," Cameron explained. "Said he doesn't want me in the clubs anymore. He feels like he'll lose me to it."

Rumor sucked her teeth. "This nigga here," she said. "What the hell does he want you to do? Stay in the house and take care of his babies like fuckin' Wilma Flinstone? Can't you have a life of your own? I swear nigga's always trying to hate on a chick's hustle. I remember when Calix tried to get me to stop dancing. Fuck that shit. It ain't nothing wrong with having your own money."

Suddenly, Cameron's curiosity got the best of her. "Where is Calix by the way...? Are ya'll taking some time apart or what?" she asked.

Rumor paused. "Yeah...he's...uh...staying with his brother for a little while in Stone Mountain."

"Oh ok."

"Anyway, enough about that loser. Let me tell you something, niggas say things like that simply 'cuz they wanna control your income. In a way, it makes them feel like they're controlling you. Don't stop dancing. You clean the house every time you climb on the pole. Shit, he ain't got no choice but to respect it at the end of the day."

Cameron added bell peppers, onion and garlic to the same pan as the chicken. "You think so?" she asked, sautéing the onions until they were tender. "I do make good money—most money I've ever made in my life to be real," she added. "But I can't go against my dude—"

"Look, he ain't gotta know if you keep strippin'," Rumor egged her on. "You can play it off like me and you are just going out to kick it. Make this paper and stack it in a separate account. That way in case anything happens you got some money to fall back on," she said. "I'm only telling you this shit because I'm your friend. Girl, your dude ain't gotta know a damn thing. He's happy and you're happy. It's as simple as that."

***

King was so impressed with Jude's little performance and showmanship of loyalty that he took him out for drinks that evening where he also promoted him in position. Instead of stealing the cars, Jude would be in charge of transporting of the vehicles. He'd make three times as much as he was making previously.

King admired the young man's perseverance and devotion—even to his piece of shit cousin—so he entrusted Jude with the responsibility, believing that he could handle it.

I am a sinner who's probably gonna sin again...

Lord forgive me, Lord forgive me things I don't understand...

Sometimes I need to be alone...

Bitch don't kill my vibe, bitch don't kill my vibe...

Jude and King sat at the bar inside of a popular downtown lounge. There were a few of King's homies with them. However, Aso had ducked off after the incident involving Vado, and Jude hadn't heard from him since.

"Someone doesn't seem as friendly today," a cute brown-skinned bartender teased before sliding a Corona in front of Jude.

There was a look of puzzlement on Jude's face. "You know me?" he asked. He didn't recognize her offhand, which was out of the ordinary since she was pretty as hell. There was no way he could forget a face like hers.

"I danced for you at Persuasion a while back at," she explained. "You had your hands all over me even though we have a strict no touching policy."

Suddenly, it dawned on Jude. "Damn, my fault, ma." He'd been so hell-bent on making Cam jealous that night that he had completely disregarded the rules. "I ain't mean to—"

"You're good," the bartender laughed. "If it really bothered me I would've said something." She then extended her hand. The rhinestones on her pink stiletto nails sparkled. "My name is Essence."

She reminded him of Kelly Rowland with twice the sex appeal and thickness. "Jude," he replied. He was surprised by how soft her hand was.

"So...Jude...do you grope all the strippers who dance for you or was I just special?" she flirted.

Jude chuckled. "Nah, I ain't really like that at all," he answered honestly. "I was...on some other shit that night. Had a lil' too much to drink. My bad about that shit. That's not how I wanna be remembered."

"But you wanna be remembered, huh?" Essence asked.

Jude laughed nervously. Essence was a beautiful woman openly flirting with him, but he was practically a married man. "I...uh...I don't know," he stammered. "So you work here and at the club?" He purposely changed the subject.

"Yep. I bartend all throughout the week and dance on the weekends," she said. "I'm also a student at Georgia Tech."

Jude nodded his head, clearly impressed. "That's what's up."

"This nigga over here harrassin' you here?" King playfully interrupted them.

"Nah, *she* the one that got *me* over here sweatin' bullets," Jude admitted.

King draped an arm around Jude's shoulder. He was drunk and high as hell. "This my mufuckin' son right here," he slurred. "Make sure you take good care of my lil' nigga tonight. He's a liability."

***

She got that million dollar...

Million dollar ooh, ooh, ooh!

Make her tap out! Tap out! Tap out!

Six coke-bottled shaped strippers—including Cameron danced on the elongated stage to "Rich Gang's *"Tapout"*. She'd completely disregarded her promise to leave the clubs alone. Just that quick Cameron had gotten used to the new lifestyle she'd adapted.

The party scene was all she was beginning to care about, and the drugs were clouding her otherwise good sense of judgment. Slowly but surely, Cameron was heading down a path of self-destruction with Rumor as the driver.

Aso sat in a VIP booth alone by himself as he watched Cameron on stage. His dick was hard was hell underneath his Troy Lee jeans. *Before it's all said and done I'ma have a taste of that shit*, he promised himself.

***

Jude walked out the lounge a couple hours later. He was feeling slightly tipsy yet his senses were still sharp. As he pulled out the keys to Cam's Audi q7, he noticed Essence standing outside against the building smoking a cigarette. He didn't know if she was taking a break or off for the night.

"You outta here?" Jude asked.

Essence blew smoke through her slightly parted lips and nodded her head. "Yeah, I've been off for about twenty minutes now," she said. "I'm waiting on my taxi. Can you believe they're talking about an hour long wait?" Essence shook her head. "Must be a busy night for 'em."

"Well, how far you stay? I don't mind giving you a ride," Jude offered.

"Oh, no. I don't wanna impose—"

"You really ain't," Jude said. "Besides, it ain't safe to be standin' out here like this. Why didn't you wait inside?"

Essence shrugged. "I get tired of being hit on," she answered. "When I punch out I don't wanna be bothered." *Except with you*, she thought to herself.

"So you want me to shoot you home real quick or you wanna wait all day for this taxi?"

Essence put out the cigarette. "Are you safe?" she asked smiling. Her bangs and long hair framed her face perfectly.

Jude cackled. "I ain't crazy or nothin' like that," he assured her. "You're in good hands..."

They both climbed into his truck which reeked of loud and Giorgio Armani cologne. Jude had a Garmin GPS mounted on the windshield to help him navigate through the new city.

"Thanks. I appreciate it," Essence said, fastening her seat belt.

"It's nothin'," Jude told her.

The ride to Essence's Camp Creek apartment was filled with small talk. She found out he was from Cleveland and worked in the 'automobile industry'. Twenty-five minutes later Jude pulled into *The Landings at Princeton Lakes*. The complex was very impressive.

"Thank you again," Essence said, unfastening her seat belt.

"How you be gettin' around with no whip?" Jude

asked. Truth be told, he wasn't ready for her to leave just yet. His buzz had him just wanting to be in the company of somebody. Anybody. And at the moment Essence was currently there.

"My car's in the shop. It should be ready for me to pick up pretty soon."

Jude nodded his head. "Truth."

"So how's Atlanta treating you?" Essence asked him.

Jude shrugged his shoulders. "It's aight," he said. "Fast-paced. But these niggas out here grind just like the niggas back at home. It's a lot alike in mo' ways than one."

Schoolboy Q's *Blessed*" played on low, creating a mellow, laid-back vibe.

"Let me see your phone," Essence said out of nowhere.

Jude gave her the side eye. "Why?"

"Just let me see your phone."

Jude handed her his cellphone.

Essence looked at the wallpaper which was a picture of Justin with a blue pacifier in his mouth. She smiled, "Aww. What a cutie. How old is he?"

"Almost two."

"Is he good?"

Jude chuckled. "Hell nah. Bad and spoiled as hell."

"Is this your only child?" Essence asked.

"That I know of," Jude laughed.

Essence didn't bother asking if he had a girl before she plugged her number into his phone and called her own. Handing him his cell back, she said, "Thanks again for the ride. Hit me up sometimes if you're looking for someone to show you the city."

Jude watched her climb out the truck, and even stole a glance at her round ass. *You don't wanna go there dawg*, he convinced himself. *If you go that route, ain't no way coming back*. After making sure Essence got into her apartment safely, Jude pulled off with no intentions of ever calling.

19

"Aye, what's up, man? Where ya ass been hiding?" Jude asked Aso. He hadn't heard from his cousin in two days so he decided to reach out.

Aso made a snorting noise and cleared his throat. He had shoved more than 0.6 grams of cocaine up his nose that afternoon, and it was nothing short of a miracle that he had yet to overdose. After years of abusing the white powder, Aso's tolerance had grown sky high. He was snorting three times as much as the typical coke user.

"Man, I just needed a few days to clear my mind," Aso snorted again. "Shit's been real hectic lately, fam."

"I can dig it, but you gotta bounce back, bro. It's still money to be made. Servin' and collectin'. That's the mission, remember?" Jude reminded him. "And Kind told me to tell you to get ya shit together. He's got some more work orders in."

"*King*?!" Aso repeated skeptically. "Fuck that power hungry mufucka. And since when do you deliver personal messages for him. Ya'll niggas gettin' a lil' too chummy lately, ain't it?"

Jude didn't miss the sarcasm in his cousin's tone. "Call it what you want...but he's payin' me big money to transport vehicles to New Jersey now." King had the stolen cars shipped out of Port Newark-Elizabeth Marine Terminal. He worked hard to make the shipment appear lawful and that's mainly where Jude came in.

Jealousy instantly washed over Aso. He had wanted

that position since he came into the business, and instead King had him running the streets looking for some damn make and models. And aside from all that, Aso had been in The Ring much longer then Jude. He was the one who'd brought cousin in.

"Oh...," was all Aso said. "Congrats...you makin' real paper now. I guess I'll get up with you later at The Warehouse." He disconnected the call before Jude could respond.

***

"Where you think you're goin'?" Jude asked Cameron the following afternoon. He'd caught her seconds before she walked out the front door.

Cameron wore a pair of Prada sunglasses and a cute floral print romper. Her short hair was cut and styled to perfection. "Me and Rumor were gonna have lunch and—"

"No you weren't," Jude cut her off. He padded over towards her, closed the front door, and took the purse out of her hand. "'Cuz me and you got plans. *Big* plans," he said.

Jude watched her expression change behind the sunglasses. "What kinda plans?"

An hour later they were running hand in hand the through Hartsfield-Jackson International Airport's parking lot. The last flight leaving out to Los Angeles departed in less than forty-five minutes and they still had to go through baggage claim.

Jude had surprised both himself and Cameron with

the impulsive decision to fly out to California. After calling up Elyse, they hastily packed, and hopped on the road to beat rush hour traffic.

Because Jude noticed the change in their relationship, he figured he had to step his game up and remind Cameron why she fell in love with him in the first place. Jude would be damned if he lost his girl to a strip club, a rapper, or even a bitch who lived next door.

Barely making it in time, Jude and Cameron were settled inside of their Delta Airlines seats ten minutes before the scheduled departure.

Cam's heart pounded rapidly in her chest as she fastened the seat belt and got comfortable. She felt a combination of nervousness, excitement, and anxiety. She'd never been on an airplane or visited the west coast a day in her life. *I can't believe we're actually doing this.*

Cameron slipped her hand in Jude's. He always found a way to be spontaneous and exciting. She never knew what his next move was, and she loved him because of that.

Suddenly, Cam's cellphone began vibrating in her lap. As expected, the caller was Rumor. Since the plane was preparing for take-off, Cameron went ahead and powered off the cell. She was with her baby, and he was the only thing that mattered.

***

Cam and Jude's plane landed in LAX at approximately 8:15 p.m. The view of the pinkish-orange sky from the terminal was absolutely beautiful, and unlike anything the two had ever seen. Palm trees lined every street and people from every shade and walks of life littered the city.

Instead of checking into their hotel immediately, the two drove to Venice Beach with the top down in a black Mercedes E350 Convertible. Kendrick Lamar's "*Poetic Justice*" flowed from the stereo, and the wind felt great blowing through Cameron's haircut.

"How did you even get the money for all this?!" she yelled over the music and loud wind.

One small lie had led to another. When she asked about his bruised hands he'd told her that he 'hurt himself on the job.' "I gotta promotion," Jude replied.

King paid Jude in advance for the transportation. Half of the money he received upfront just for making the drive. The rest he got when the car was safely inside the shipping container.

"I can't believe I'm in Cali!" Cameron said excitedly. Being there felt so surreal, almost as if it were a dream.

Jude laughed as he navigated the car. Pulling out his cellphone, he opened the video and turned it towards Cam. "Scream that shit, bay."

Cameron anxiously tossed her hands in the air. "*WOOOOO!* I'm in Cali, bitches!"

***

Cameron and Jude walked hand in hand on the shore of Venice Beach. The sand was so warm between their toes, and the fact that it was night time made it seem even more breathtaking. The colorful amusement park's light lit up the beach and there were even a few fireworks—even though it was nowhere near close to being the Fourth of July.

"I can't believe me and you are here right here," Cameron said. "You really took me by surprise with this one."

Jude wrapped an arm around her shoulder and pulled her close. "I gotta keep it fresh," he told her. "Keep you guessin'. If our relationship has some spontaneity you'll never get bored with a nigga."

Cameron wrapped her arm around Jude's waist. "Boy, I will *never* get bored with you," she told him. Of course, she's been feeling O' Zone a little but that didn't mean she had lost interest in her man. "Do you think Justin will be fine with Elyse for a couple days? We've never left him with her so long," she suddenly asked.

"He's good," Jude reassured her. "Now stop worryin'. We're in Los Angeles."

***

Cameron stared at the city's skyline from inside of her hotel room while wearing nothing but a Jonquil Eve silk robe. They had chosen to stay in The Ritz-Carlton located in downtown LA. Jude was dropping nearly $600 a night for them to crash in the king bedroom overlooking the city, but it was all worth it when it came to Cameron.

It was then that she felt Jude wrap his arms around her from behind. He placed soft kisses on the side of her neck. When Cameron looked down she noticed a red velvet box in his hands.

"What's this?" she asked.

"Open it," Jude whispered.

Cameron's heart thumped wildly inside her chest. With steady fingers she lifted the lid to the small jewelry box. Inside was a sparkling 14k white gold diamond engagement ring. The glistening carats reflected off her dark lenses.

"Jude...I—How—"

"Tell me yes again, baby girl." Jude kissed Cameron's shoulder then her neck. "Make this night memorable by tellin' me yes one more time..."

Cameron turned around and faced Jude. "Yes! Yes! Of course!"

Jude moved his dreads out of his face so that he could see himself slip the ring on Cameron's ringer. "If these niggas out here don't know...now they will..." He leaned down and gently pressed his lips against hers.

Cameron eagerly slipped her tongue inside Jude's warm mouth and wrapped her arms around his neck.

In one swift motion, Jude lifted Cameron up and placed her on the cream down comforter since it was the closest thing nearby. He carefully sat her down in an upright position before getting onto his knees, and spreading her thick thighs.

Cameron watched intently as he buried his head between her legs. In the dark room, the only thing she could see were the whites of Jude's eyes as he stared up at her.

Cameron bit her bottom lip as spread her legs farther apart, and allowed him to slide his wet tongue from her pussy to her asshole. "Oh, my goodness, baby…," she moaned breathlessly.

Jude held one of her legs back, and with his free hand massaged her soft breast. "You gon' always be mine?" he asked before gently biting her inner thigh.

"Yes! God, yes!"

Jude brought her foot toward his mouth, and ran his tongue along each and every toe before nibbling on her heel.

Cameron moaned as she slipped her own two fingers inside her slippery pussy. Jude continued to work his tongue magic on her perfect toes, and when foreplay was no longer enough he slid inside.

Taking Cameron's moist fingers in his mouth, Jude sucked off her wetness. He then slipped his tongue inside her mouth so she could taste herself. Young and madly in love, the two expressed their affection for one another with amorous love-making sessions.

Jude delicately turned Cameron over on the sofa and penetrated her from behind. Holding onto her shapely hips for support, he used them to guide his deep strokes.

Cam whimpered as he hit her spot repeatedly. Jude knew her body like the back of his hand.

She tossed her head back in pure pleasure. Jude suckled and nibbled on her flesh as he massaged her slippery clit. Cameron wrapped her arm around Jude's neck from behind, and tried her best to push it back on him. His abdominal muscles flexed with each stroke.

"I wanna feel you bust on this dick, Cam," Jude

coached her. "This my pussy?"

"Fuck yes!"

Jude grabbed a handful of Cam's short curly hair, and pounded ferociously into her from behind. He was trying to make a point more than anything. "Damn right. These niggas out here ain't gon' fuck you like I do."

Cameron's cheeks grew hotter. "Ooh, I love when you talk that shit, Jude!" she cried out. "Damn, I'm about to cum."

That was all the incentive Jude needed. "Cum then, babe," he said. "You know I ain't lettin' go 'til you do."

Moments later, they released simultaneously before collapsing onto the down comforter. "Shit, Cam," Jude said, panting heavily. "You done made a nigga fall in love all over again..."

Cameron took Jude's moist, flaccid penis in her mouth and sucked him until he was rock hard again. "I didn't know it was possible to fall in love twice," she said, straddling his dick.

"I didn't either..."

20

The next day Jude took Cameron on Rodeo Drive where she shopped all the designer labels and brands. By the time she finished her mini-shopping spree, Cameron carried bags from Chanel, Giuseppe Zanotti, and Prada.

Jude and Cameron looked like a young celebrity couple as they traipsed inside designer stores and walked out toting bags. Cameron had only dreamed about moments like this. Yet sadly, she still had no idea about the details of Jude's occupation.

***

Knock! Knock! Knock!

Aso rapped softly on King's office door and waited patiently for an answer. Dark bags rested underneath his hazel eyes. He didn't even look like himself. Lana's death and the unexpected situation with Vado were taking a drastic toll on him.

Lana's parents had called the house a few times after claiming that they hadn't spoken to her in weeks. He wondered if they knew about her plotting to have them killed for an inheritance would have made them less concerned about their daughter. Either way, it would only be a matter of time before police began snooping and asking questions. Aso needed to make some real paper so that he could get ghost.

"Come in," King said dryly.

Aso quietly opened the door and stepped inside. "What's up, man? I know you busy and shit, but I just had to holla at you 'bout somethin' real quick."

King peeled his attention off the fraudulent car title paperwork on his deck, and looked over at Aso. "What's good?" There were no emotions in his tone, and Aso could tell he didn't want to be bothered.

"Jude told me you put him in charge of transporting the vehicles," Aso began. "No offense, but I think that's lightweight fucked up considerin' I been in this game way longer than him—"

"So lemme get this right," King interrupted him. "You comin' in my office questionin' my decision-makin' I make in *my* business? Is that what I'm hearin'?"

Aso thought about the way King savagely beat Vado with his leather belt. Holding his hands up in mock surrender, he said, "I ain't tryin' to come at you like that at all, man—"

"Then what the fuck you complainin' about?" King asked in a nasty tone. "Don't I pay you good money to do what you do? Shit, judgin' from gear you wear and the Maserati you pushin' I'd say you're makin' out just fine. You heard me?"

King estimated the total cost of Aso's outfit to be nearly $5,000. His spiked cheetah print Louboutin sneakers had to have been worth well over a thousand dollars.

"But it ain't even about that—"

"Then what the fuck is it about?" King asked. He intertwined his fingers and studied Aso from behind his desk. "'Cuz from my perspective it looks like you bargin' up in my office talkin' 'bout a whole bunch of nothin'. I was diggin' ya cuz's swag and I thought he'd be good with the responsibility. It is what is—"

"So you sayin' you couldn't have trusted me?" Aso argued. "Bruh, I been rockin' with you for years." He was really taking it personally.

King shook his head. "You still got so much shit to learn..."

***

The exuberance from the Cali trip was short-lived, and as soon as Jude and Cam got back to Georgia things went right back to being the same. The only difference now was that Cameron had a ring on her finger. Jude went back to working for King, and Cameron went back to partying with Rumor and O' Zone.

With Jude hustling and becoming better acquainted with King and his empire, Cameron and Rumor were busy being the life of the party. Jude was completely oblivious to the fact that his girl was still dancing behind his back. Cameron knew he would be disappointed in her going against him, but she just couldn't stay away. The clubs were like an addiction.

Instead of spending time and taking care of her only child, Cameron chose to continue to dump the responsibility on Elyse. She was beginning to feel like she had better things to do than being a housewife and full-time mom. The streets were calling her and Cam just couldn't ignore them.

Cameron also couldn't ignore O' Zone's calls, text messages, and the immense effort he was putting in to get her attention. She still had yet to tell him that she had a man, so the ambitious artist couldn't figure out why she insisted on bullshitting and playing games with her. Cam was worth it, but she was making him work harder than he'd ever had to work in his life.

Jude had grown incredibly close to King over the last few weeks. It seemed like the cooler he got with his boss/mentor the further apart he and Aso grew apart. Since tensions were at an all-time high between them, Jude moved Cam and Justin out of Aso's midtown townhome and into a beautiful 3 bedroom 2 ½ bathroom home. King was the one who put the deposit down on the house.

The impressive in-town home had a historical charm with modern updates. The entire house was wired for surround sound, and it also featured crown molding, and hardwood floors throughout. The rent came in at a whopping $3500 a month, but no expense was too great for Jude when it came to his family.

There weren't a lot of niggas King fooled with. He used a long-handled spoon whenever dealing with most people because he didn't trust too many motherfuckers, especially around his family. However, Jude was different. He gave his boss a good vibe. King even called him his son although he was only ten years older than Jude at thirty-four. He was more like a big brother/father figure to his twenty-four year old protégée.

Jude had gotten so close with King that his boss invited him to his home for a cookout one bright and sunny afternoon. King's six-bedroom, seven-bathroom mini mansion looked like a house off of MTV's Cribs. The gorgeous lot sat on nearly two acres of land and overlooked a golf course.

His cookout mostly consisted of family and close business associates. He introduced Jude to his wife, Katrina and his seven-year old daughter. In turn King met Cam and Justin.

Cameron assumed she was meeting her fiancé's manager. She figured King and Jude's close business relationship stemmed from hard work and building a rapport. The "business trips" Jude took seemed legitimate enough so Cameron's suspicions were never raised.

Hip hop music played on maximum in the back of King's conventional home. Hired chefs and bartenders held down the full outdoor kitchen and bar. A few individuals sat underneath the gazebo chatting and sipping while others took to the large swimming pool.

"Damn, we just keep runnin' into each other, huh?" Tank took off his Gucci glasses and smiled at Cameron.

She sat in a poolside chair with her son, minding her business. "Lucky me, huh?" she asked, her tone dripping with sarcasm. She then looked over at Jude who looked to be in deep conversation with King.

"Damn, it ain't nothin' like that, ma," Tank said, noticing her look in her man's direction. "I ain't tryin' to get you in trouble. Plus that's fam. I ain't that nigga."

Cameron forced a phony smile.

"Just wanted to say what's up and good luck. Ya'll make a good couple."

"Bye Tank," Cameron waved.

Tank chuckled, and shook his head before walking away.

Aso stood off to the side with a hating ass expression as he watched King and Jude talk near the pool. Jealousy coursed through his veins because of the favoritism. Instead of being happy that his cousin had made a come up, Aso was instead envious.

I'm the one who brought this nigga into the circle and now he's stealing all my damn shine.

Aso then noticed Cameron sitting in a poolside chair with her son Justin by her side. She wore a blue sea ombre swimsuit and a pair of round sunglasses. His dirty thoughts were interrupted when Tank suddenly approached him. He'd purposely stayed away to let the situation die down. Today was actually their first time running into each other since their last conversation.

"What's good?" Tank greeted Aso.

Aso pretended he didn't see his brother as he continued to chew on a toothpick.

"Really though? You gon' act like we kids or some shit?"

Aso finally looked at Tank. "You foul as fuck, nigga."

Tank shook his head in disagreement. "Nah, I honestly think you should be thanking me. I opened ya eyes. That bitch was no good—and her pussy wasn't all that either—"

Aso shoved the hell out of Tank.

Everyone immediately stopped what they were

doing to watch the altercation near the pool. Jude and King rushed over before a full own brawl broke out.

"Ya'll niggas need to chill. Ya'll makin' a mufuckin' scene." King told them. "Now this ain't the place for that bullshit."

Tank pointed at Aso. "This fuck nigga over here cryin' over pussy and shit—"

The unexpected blow sent Tank crashing into an outdoor table. It took his brain a moment to realize that Aso had just punched him. Forgetting that he was his brother, Tank tackled him with full force. Both brothers landed on the concrete with a thug.

A few other guys rushed over to pull the two apart.

"Fuck you bitch nigga!" Aso spat. "It wasn't enough for you to fuck Jude's girl! You had to fuck mine too, huh?"

Jude turned and looked at Tank. *"You fucked Cam?!"*

TAT! TAT! TAT! TAT! TAT! TAT! TAT!

The sound of an AK 47 going off caused people to scream and scatter frantically. Some people were smart enough to duck down in order to avoid being caught in gunfire. Others pushed and shoved each other to get out.

Glass shattered as bullets whizzed from every direction. Two random people were struck were hit in gunfire.

Cameron hastily dropped to the ground and tried her best to shield Justin. Crouching down, Jude sprinted over towards his girl and child, trying his best to avoid being shot. Unfortunately, he didn't have his piece on him at the time.

Apparently, Mitch—the man whom King had killed—was causing more problems dead than alive. His brother and cousin squeezed off rounds into the cookout wearing nothing but black attire and ski masks. They didn't give a damn that it was broad daylight or that they were in a quiet, upscale Alpharetta neighborhood.

A cookout that started off normal had quickly turned into gunfire and chaos.

King shielded his daughter's body after taking cover behind the outdoor bar. Luckily his wife was inside and out of harm's way. "Get them mufuckas!" he yelled to two of his boys.

But it was too late. The masked gunmen took off running towards the front of the house before hopping into a black Escalade with tinted windows. King's goons chased after them with their own weapons drawn, but the truck skirted off before they could bust any shots.

Cameron's entire body trembled uncontrollably, and Justin continued to cry at the top of his lungs. A few people felt comfortable enough to come out of their hiding spots before taking in the damage.

One of the victims caught in gunfire lay face down in the crystal blue pool water. A dime-sized bullet hole was in the center of his back.

"Are you okay?" Jude asked with concern in his voice. He cupped her face in his hands. There were tears in her eyes as she held Justin against her chest.

Cameron sniffled and wiped her nose. "Yeah...I— I think I'm good," she stuttered.

Cameron's eyes slowly wandered to the blood soaking Jude's t-shirt. "Oh, my God! You're bleeding!"

21

Tears pooled Aso's eyes as he crawled over toward Tank who lay outstretched on the concrete. A small puddle of blood slowly formed around his immobile body.

"Bruh...?" Aso croaked out. "Bruh, get up." Tears spilled over his lower lids as he looked down at his dead brother. He placed his hand over the gunshot in the center of Tank's chest as if to stop the bleeding. However, the effort was useless. His brother was gone. "Say something," Aso cried. "Get up!"

Jude held onto his side as he jogged over to Aso and Tank. Fortunately, he'd only been grazed by a stray bullet.

"Man, them mufuckas killed my brotha!" Aso screamed.

Chills ran up Cameron's spine after hearing the pain in Aso's voice. She then looked over at King who was making sure his daughter was okay.

***

"You're quiet...," Jude noted as they left North Fulton Hospital. Fifteen stitches and a brief conversation with the police was the outcome of the shooting. "You sure you're good?"

Cameron didn't respond until they were inside their truck. Thankfully, Justin had fallen asleep. "Why do you think that happened?" she finally asked.

Cam didn't particularly like Tank too much, but

she also hated to see his life end the way it did. There was no way she'd be able to sleep peacefully after everything that happened that day. The EMTs had to pry Aso off his brother in order to get his body on a stretcher and inside the ambulance. Two people had been gunned and a total of four—including Jude—had been injured.

Cameron couldn't see any other reason why two guys would run up in a cook out on some Columbine shit unless…

"I told you already—just like I told the police—it was a random shootin'," Jude said with irritation in tone. "Nobody knows why those niggas came up bustin'. This is a crazy world. People do fucked up shit, Cam."

"But—"

"Cam, come on now. I really ain't in the mood to keep talkin' 'bout this shit," he cut her off. "I just lost my fuckin' cousin…"

Cameron settled back into her seat, and decided to drop the subject for now, at least. She knew sooner or later she'd find out the truth.

***

Two days after Tank's death Aso sat on the hood on his car while sipping a bottle of Hennessey. Family and friends had been blowing his phone up since he got the news but he really didn't want to be bothered. Mentally, he'd snapped. He didn't give a damn about anything or anyone else. He was out for himself, and he didn't give a damn who he'd have to betray.

***

Tank's death seemingly caused an even bigger rift in Jude and Aso's relationship. Aso barely acted as if he wanted to speak to his cousin when Jude offered condolences at the funeral which was held back in their hometown. King had even flown down to pay his respect. There was also a change in Jude and Cameron's relationship. He was a little disheartened about her sleeping with Tank and not telling him about it even though she swore it was years ago.

Their relationship was nowhere near close to being perfect, but it wasn't bad enough to make either of them leave. The tension in their household however was undeniable. The closer Jude got to King and his job, the further he pushed Cam away.

Cameron, on the other hand, wasn't doing much to correct the situation. The less attention Jude paid her the more she sought it in the streets. She and Rumor had gotten extremely close, and she'd hung out with O' Zone on numerous occasions. Nothing had popped off as of yet, and Cam never intended for anything to happen. She loved Jude very much, and he never had a single reason not to trust Cameron...until he ran into Aso one afternoon. It was the first time they'd spoken since Tank's funeral.

Jude was collecting the last of his belongings from Aso's townhome when the two crossed paths. Aso tried his best to make it look like running into his cousin was a coincidence. The truth was he couldn't wait to show Jude the video he'd stumbled upon while browsing through his newsfeed on Instagram.

Aso tried to play it off like he was looking out for Jude when in all actuality he was purposely trying to hurt him. Jude and Cameron should've been him and Lana...but unfortunately things didn't go as planned. Instead of being happy for his cousin, he was trying to secretly sabotage him in any way that he could.

"What's good, fam?" Aso dapped Jude up. "You just the mufucka I been lookin' for."

Jude placed a small cardboard box in the trunk of his metallic blue BMW 335is.

Jealousy consumed Aso after seeing the new car. It had nothing to do with whose ride was better than the other. He was just upset about Jude making a come-up that he felt he deserved.

"When you cop that, cuz?" Aso asked, masking his resentment.

"Oh, this? King actually gave it to me," Jude said nonchalantly.

Aso was salty-faced after hearing that. *That mothafucka ain't never gave me shit and I been stealing whips for this nigga for years*, he seethed. Instead of being happy to see his cousin shining, he was hating like a motherfucker on the low.

"It's dope," Aso lied.

Jude slammed the trunk close and turned towards his older cousin. "So anyway, what's good, man? How you been feelin' lately? You straight?" There was genuine concern in his eyes as he waited for a response. "You know you ain't the only one who lost a brother," he said. "I know that shit cuts deep, man."

Aso waved him. "Yeah, I'm good. I'm good," he

forced a weak smile. Most days he tried not to even think about his brother. The stress of Lana's parents hounding him about their daughter's whereabouts had quickly become more important.

"Well, you know if you ever wanna chop it, I'm here."

"Cool. Cool. I appreciate that." Aso dapped up Jude, and for two seconds he almost stopped resenting him. Almost.

"So what you had to tell me?" Jude asked.

Aso pulled out his cellphone. "It ain't what I gotta tell you," he corrected Jude. "It's what I gotta *show* you." He leaned against Jude's BMW, and pulled up a video on O' Zone's personal Instagram page.

Confused but still curious, Jude leaned in and looked at Aso's cellphone screen. "Hell is this?" he asked.

Aso didn't reply. He decided to let the video clip speak for itself.

"This how we mufuckin' do it out here in the ATL, shawty! We turn up to the mufuckin' sun rise, nigga! Who fuckin' with Greek Gang ENT? Not a na'an nigga! Get wit' it or get run the fuck over!"

Jude's expression slowly fluctuated into anger as he watched Cameron party with the popular, upcoming rapper and his posse. He was shocked beyond belief when he saw her snort an unrecognizable powdery substance. He almost didn't recognize his girl.

Jude squeezed the car keys tightly in his hand as he watched O' Zone playfully spin Cam around. Her laughter—and the fact that it looked like she was enjoying herself—made him feel sick to his stomach.

Damn. It's like that?

Embarrassed was an understatement. Cameron was supposed to be his woman—his wife—and yet she was out partying and getting high with other niggas when her ass should have been at home taking care of their son.

Jude's jaw muscle tensed as he stared at the phone's small screen. He was tempted to snatch it and throw it as far as he possibly could. Yet he knew the images would forever remain his mind.

Jude thought back to her promising him that he'd never have to doubt her. Anger quickly built up inside of him, and he felt like a volcano preparing to erupt.

"I really ain't wanna show you at first," Aso said. "But I figured if the shoe was on the other foot I'd wanna know. You know what I mean?"

Jude nodded his head. "Good lookin', man. I'ma get up with you later. Be easy," was all he said before hopping in his BMW. His somber body language was enough to make Aso crack a smirk behind his cousin's back.

22

Cameron rolled her eyes in irritation as she tried to concentrate on applying the RiRi Woo lipstick. Justin hollered at the top of his little lungs inside his bedroom. Cam wasn't sure what her son was fussing about, but she was too busy getting ready to check on him. Ironically, Cameron used to chastise Pocahontas about neglecting her daughter, and now she was doing the exact same thing with her son. Somehow she'd gotten off track, and forgot about what was really important: her family.

After spraying on a few squirts of Oscar de la Renta perfume, she tossed back a pill, and washed it down with the shot glass of Hen sitting on the bathroom counter. Rumor had the hookup on all types of illegal meds thanks to the pharmacist who issued the meds for her sickness. She tossed him a few bills here and there, and he took care of her needs like a dealer serving a fiend.

"Elyse?!" Cameron yelled out. "Justin's crying!"

"I'm sorry, I'm coming now!" Elyse shouted from downstairs.

After mashing her lips together, Cameron mumbled, "Damn, bitch. What am I paying you for?"

Her change in character was so drastic, and out of control that she didn't even see herself spiraling.

An hour later, Cameron and Rumor were inside of Zeus' luxurious basement studio lounging and enjoying the session. Rumor's head rested in Cam's lap while her feet were propped up on the arm of the sofa. She took a few short pulls on a blunt and handed it to her best friend.

O' Zone was going at it in the recording room, feeling himself as he let his lyrics flow off the top of his head.

"...She claim she tired of the same shit. Same dick. Need a boss nigga that ain't gone take her shit, and pay her rent. But what about when all my money spent? Would you still hold me down? Say she ain't met a nigga this real since her pops was around. She a Midwest chick. Straight reckless. And her head game is epic. Got me competing with her exes..."

Suddenly, Cameron was distracted when her cellphone began vibrating. After seeing Jude's name flash across her screen, Cameron crept out of the studio and went upstairs. Framed pictures of Zeus with many of ATL's hottest celebs decorated one of the walls.

"Hey, babe," Cameron answered.

"I see you ain't at home—as usual," Jude spat. "So where the fuck you at?"

Cameron was caught off guard by his unfriendly tone. "With Rumor. Why?" she asked.

"Bring yo' ass home," he demanded. "We need to talk ASAP."

"Well, I'm busy right now," she argued.

"I'm not finna ask yo' ass again, Cameron," Jude said. "Come. Home. Now." He paused between each word to let her know how serious he was.

"I left the truck at home," Cam quickly said. "I rode with Rumor, and I doubt she's trying to leave anytime soon." Honestly, she was enjoying herself too much leave. At only twenty-one, Cameron found much more excitement in the streets than being the little housewife Jude wanted her to be. She was losing herself in the thrill of adventures.

"Aight, then...I see what it is," Jude told her. "You gon' 'head and do whatever the hell you want. Fuck you, you ungrateful ass bitch." CLICK!

***

Just 'cuz she loves me, don't mean she understands...

I don't give a damn, I'll make her fuck the band...

I already know. I've seen her at my show banging out XO...

And her friend's a freak...She can't feel her throat...She can't feel her knees...

And I'm not tryna talk...And I'm not tryna walk...

Just lift me out the club...

Cameron's head felt like it was swimming as she sat in the passenger of O' Zone's red Audi r8 with the top down. A combination of drinking, smoking, and popping 2 mg of

Rumor had gone off to work, and for once it was just the two of them. They cruised through the metropolitan city, trying to figure out their next move while listening to music and shooting the breeze. Cam hadn't even tried to call Jude back and make up with him, nor did he with her.

O' Zone reached over and lowered the volume to

the music. "Shit, I almost forgot. I'm the special guest host tonight at Reign. You tryin' to slide through with a nigga?" he asked. "You know I can't miss an opportunity to show yo' ass off."

Cameron shrugged. "Sounds cool," she said, looking out at the passing scenery. "It's not like I have anything else to do....or anyone else to be with," she added cynically.

O' Zone gave her bare thigh a firm squeeze. "That ain't 'til after midnight though," he explained. "So how 'bout we get into somethin' before then? As a matter of fact, I can think of somethin' I wouldn't mind gettin' into right now."

The Weeknd crooned on the audio system, and Cam couldn't have agreed anymore.

It's gon' be one of those nights...

***

Jude could have gone to any bar he wanted to in or near the city, however, he chose to have a drink at the one Essence worked at. *Back-ups stay on deck. Fuck this bitch thought*, he said to himself.

Essence smiled and waved at Jude the moment she saw him walk over towards the bar. He got fresh too death that night just to step out solo. Wearing a Givenchy shirt, fitted denim jeans, and red leather Louboutin sneakers, Jude grabbed the attention of almost every woman in the place—even the ones who were with their men.

The Breitling Bentley watched glimmered around his wrist, and his freshly twisted dreads were pulled back neatly.

"How're you doin', sweetie?" Essence greeted him.

Jude smiled. "Better now..."

***

O' Zone lived in a deluxe sky rise condo in the heart of downtown Atlanta. The 2,428 square foot two-bedroom apartment home included a den as well as a terrace which offered a magnificent view of the city.

The den was where O' Zone and Cameron chose to lounge. The expansive room was every man's fantasy. A small stage and metal pole sat positioned in the middle of the room. Colorful strobe lights hung overhead. Tiny, circular specks of colors rolled across the ceiling and walls, giving the den an almost club-like feel. A bar was stationed in the back of the room, and the Bose home theater ran O' Zone nearly a grand.

"Well, don't just sit there, shawty. Get up and dance for me or somethin'. Entertain a nigga, shit. You got me 'bout damn ready to fall asleep on ya ass," O' Zone joked. He reached over and placed his hand over hers. The $26,000 diamond ring on his right finger glistened.

Higher than the Hubble Space Telescope, Cameron sat on the cream Anastacia Pearl Sofa, practically nodding off herself. "Put some music on then," she murmured. "And pull out some cash."

O' Zone stood to his feet, dug into his jeans pocket, and pulled out a thick wad of cash. "Oh, money ain't a thang, shawty. Believe that," he said with a blunt dangling out the corner of his mouth. "I'm still tryin' to figure out how the fuck a nigga fit 30K in one pocket."

O' Zone loved to boast and show off his success. Struggling and clawing his way to the top, it felt great having money to fuck off whenever he felt like it. After living twenty-plus years broke as hell, O' Zone wanted the world to know and see he was paid. Getting his chain snatched after one of his concerts wasn't enough to dissuade him in the least. After the incident, he flexed even harder, but had twice as much security with him.

O' Zone swaggered over towards the audio system and turned it on. Tiara Thomas' voice immediately serenaded Cameron as she slowly stood to her feet.

Is it bad that I never made love, no I never did it…

But I sure know how to fuck…

I'll be your bad girl, I'll prove it to you…

I can't promise that I'll be good to you…

"Are you serious?" Cameron smiled.

O' Zone plopped down on the sofa and enjoyed the performance as he lit up another blunt. "Yeah…show me what you do…"

Cameron grabbed the pole and began swaying with the music. She was in a zone as she let the melody take over her body movements.

"Come up out dem clothes," O' Zone said.

Cameron did a slow, seductive twirl around the pole. "The more money I see, the more clothes I take off…"

O' Zone tossed a handful of bills in her direction. There were no ones in the knot. Only tens, twenties, and fifties. "Like I said, money ain't a thang for a nigga like me."

Bad girls ain't no good, and the good girls ain't no fun...

And the hood girls want a smart nigga, college girls all want a thug...

Cameron pulled the striped long-sleeved crop top over her head and tossed it on the floor. The colorful strobe lights danced on her smooth, honey skin.

O' Zone nodded his head in admiration and grabbed his erection through his jeans. Licking his lips, he continued to watch her tease him with a strip show.

Cameron ran her hands enticingly down her midsection. If not anything else she was pro at being a seductress.

O' Zone threw more money in her direction.

As promised, Cameron wiggled out of the acid wash pencil skirt. Dressed in nothing but a Victoria's Secret lilac panty and bra set, she rolled her stomach and hips with the beat.

O' Zone's dick was ready to burst through the seams as he watched her dance. After the song ended and the next played he had finally had enough of the games and stalling. Curling his finger, O' Zone beckoned Cameron to come closer.

Smiling mischievously, she sashayed towards him and climbed into his lap. His erection pressed into her, and she already knew what he wanted.

"When you gon' stop playin' and be mine?" O' Zone asked, grabbing her round, soft booty.

"You know I'm already someone else's…"

O' Zone sucked his teeth. "Man, fuck that nigga you dealin' with. He ain't 'bout shit—I mean, look where you at right now. With me," he pointed out. "Say the shit with me…'Fuck him'."

Cameron thought about her and Jude's earlier conversation. She kept hearing his angry voice in the back of her mind calling her an ungrateful ass bitch. His harsh choice of words really hurt her deeply.

O' Zone cupped Cameron's chin and tilted her head towards him. "Say the shit with me, babe," he repeated. "Fuck him."

"You gon' 'head and do whatever the hell you want. Fuck you, you ungrateful ass bitch."

"Fuck him," Cameron finally said in a low tone.

O' Zone smiled. "That's my bitch," he said before kissing her.

23

    After clocking out for the evening, Jude treated Essence to dinner at California Dreaming since she claimed they had the best chicken salads. Following the meal, the two headed back downtown to have drinks at *Wet Willies*. When they were full and tipsy off strawberry daiquiris, Essence insisted upon taking Jude onto the city's giant Skyview Ferris Wheel.

    "I don't really fuck with heights, ma," Jude told Essence.

    Essence grabbed his hand and pulled him in the direction of the 200-foot Ferris wheel. "Don't be a scary cat," she said. "Come on! It'll be fun!"

***

    "Why you over there sittin' lookin' like you ain't havin' fun?" O' Zone asked. He reached over and pinched one of Cameron's dark brown nipples.

    They had just finished having sex, and Cameron now felt like total shit. At first, she thought sleeping with O' Zone was what she wanted, but now she regretted it more than someone not taking their credit seriously. Cameron would never be able to undo this shit. *What the hell did I just do?* She stared at her engagement ring. It sparkled on her finger, reminding her of the commitment and promise she'd made.

    O' Zone continued writhing Cameron's hardened nipple between his fingers until she suddenly slapped his hand away. "Leave me alone," she said coolly. "I don't wanna be touched right now." He was the last person she wanted to be bothered with.

"Fuck wrong witchu?" O'Zone asked. "You mad I made that pussy cum?"

Cameron looked away as tears formed in her eyes.

O' Zone climbed out the California king-sized espresso bed and stood to his feet. His chest was covered in tiny beads of sweat from an aggressive sex session. "Well, fuck you too then," he retaliated before walking off.

When O' Zone slammed the bedroom door behind him, Cameron was happy to finally be alone. Now that she was sober she was fully aware of her emotions and guilt. She felt horrible. There she was...a woman practically married sleeping with a man she practically knew nothing about.

Cameron drew her knees to her chest and sobbed quietly. *What the hell am I doing? This isn't even me. This isn't me at all.*

After wiping her tears, Cameron grabbed her cellphone off the nightstand and called Jude's cellphone number.

***

Jude and Essence shared great conversation and even a few laughs as they sat inside the closed in seats on the Skyview Ferris Wheel. Seeing the city's skyline was unlike anything Jude had ever experienced. It was remarkable.

I should be doing shit like this with Cam, Jude

thought to himself. However, lately Cameron had been pushing him away to run the streets instead. Then again, he wasn't any better. Making regular trips to and from New Jersey kept him pretty busy. Truthfully, Jude had been lacking in his commitment as well, and aside from the Cali trip, he and Cameron hadn't done anything else special since.

Surprisingly, Essence actually made for great company. She listened, she was smart, and she was pretty.

You'd take the clothes off my back and I'd let you...

You'd steal the food right out my mouth and I'd watch you eat it...

I still don't know why, why I love you so much...

The unexpected ringing of Jude's cellphone interrupted their conversation about traveling. When he saw Cameron's picture flash across the screen, he contemplated on whether or not to answer. *Which one should I press? The lime or the red?*

After finally making a decision, Jude pressed the ignore button. Essence had Jude's full attention for that evening. If Cameron wanted to do her he would do him as well.

"My fault about that," Jude apologized before powering off his cellphone.

Essence gave him a million-dollar smile. "You gotta different type of swag, Jude," she confessed. "I can't put my finger on it...but you're different than a lot of these other guys."

"Is that good?" he asked.

Essence scooted closer. "I like it...," she said, leaning in for a kiss.

Jude moved back slightly, avoiding her plump lips by a few centimeters.

Essence immediately felt embarrassed. She was unsure of what she had done wrong. *Damn, maybe it's too early*, she thought to herself. "Oh...um...My fault. I—I thought—"

Jude leaned in and kissed Essence. When he felt her warm tongue slide inside his mouth he quickly pulled back and cleared his throat nervously. If he didn't end it there, he'd surely do something he would regret later.

"Let me get you back home," Jude said.

***

"Aye, my bad about that shit." O' Zone joined her in the bedroom ten minutes after his outburst. He carried a small silver tray as he made his way towards the bed.

Cameron already knew what it was before she even saw the contents on top of it.

"Do a couple lines with me before we leave," O' Zone offered. "Just enough to heal ya problems...too much will kill ya," he said, quoting one of Drake's infamous lines.

***

Jude pulled into *The Landings at Princeton Lakes*, and circled around the beautiful apartment complex until he arrived at Essence's buildings. After parking, he left the car on and hopped out. Like the gentleman he was raised to be, Jude opened the passenger door for her.

"Thank you," she said.

"No prob. I enjoyed chillin' witchu today," Jude told her.

Essence stood on her tip toes and gently pressed her lips against his. "I enjoyed your company too," she whispered. "Now let's not let the night end here..."

Jude was surprised by her straightforwardness. She took his hand in hers and attempted to lead the way to her apartment unit—however, Jude wouldn't budge.

Essence turned around and gave him a puzzled look. There was a humorless expression on his handsome face. "What's up?" she asked, laughing.

"I can't do that with you, ma" Jude said in a serious tone. "To keep it real, I just got engaged..."

Disappointment immediately swept over Essence. "Oh," she said flatly. "Well...thanks for leading me on only to *keep it real*." Sarcasm oozed from her voice.

Jude sighed in defeat. "Man, my fault, Essence. I should've been straight up with you," he apologized.

Essence waved him off. She tried her best to hide her embarrassment. "No, it's cool. Really it is," she said. "Good luck with that, Jude. I wish you the best." Essence forced a weak smile and headed in the direction of her apartment building. *All the good ones are always taken*, she thought.

Feeling like an even bigger asshole, Jude trudged towards his BMW.

Essence turned on her heel and faced Jude. "If she messes up and you happen to venture back into 'singles' territory—"

"You'll be the first to know," Jude promised.

***

Cameron sat silent in the VIP room beside Rumor as she nodded her head to the beat of Travis Scott's "*Upper Echelon.*" She had agreed to come and show her support, but the longer she sat inside Reign Night Club the more she didn't really want to be there.

Zeus sat in a plush red, leather booth across from them, but he wasn't paying either of them any attention. He was instead focused on the dance floor.

A fruit flavored hookah laced with weed sat on the table in front them along with an ice bucket sheltering an expensive bottle of champagne. Cameron should have been having fun, and turning up with her new friend, but she looked more bored than a kid in church.

Rumor, on the other hand, looked like she was enjoying herself as she danced in the VIP room. However, when she saw the boredom on Cameron's face she slid in the booth beside her.

"Ugh, bitch, why you sitting over here like you don't wanna be bothered?" Rumor nudged Cameron's shoulder. She looked alluring that evening in a black mesh bodysuit which revealed her bulging cleavage, hips, and thighs. "Have a drink or something. You fuckin' up my flow with ya sobriety."

Cameron shook her head. "I don't really feel like drinking, Rumor" she said.

"Well, sober hoe, come into the bathroom with

me real quick."

Cameron and Rumor wiggled out of the VIP booth and made their way downstairs to the public restrooms. Once inside, Rumor pulled a small plastic bag from her purse containing miniscule pills.

Cameron's nose was still slightly numb from the junk she'd shoved up in it earlier. "Girl, I really don't feel like takin—"

"Shut up, close your eyes, and stick your tongue out," Rumor said.

Cameron blew out air and did as instructed. She felt like a total fool as she stood in the women's restroom with her eyes shut tight, and her skinny pink tongue sticking halfway out.

Rumor placed a tiny white pill on the tip of Cameron's tongue. "That should be enough to make you have fun but still keep you mellow," she said. "So how was it?".

"I don't know. It's too early to tell," Cameron answered.

"No, bitch, not the pill. I'm talking about O' Zone," Rumor said. "Did he put it on you?"

Cameron walked over to the restroom's mirror and reapplied her MAC lipstick. "I don't wanna talk about we did. I still have a hard time I actually did the shit. What am I gonna tell Jude?"

"Why do you have to tell that nigga anything?" Rumor asked. "Fuck him. He ain't gotta know. I mean, your dude's cool and all but he ain't no O' Zone. You need to quit playing and drop that zero and get with a boss."

Cameron narrowed her eyes at Rumor through the restroom mirror. "Rumor, I just can't leave my man for a fantasy. Me and Jude have history. We've stayed by each other's side through hard times...we've overcome obstacles together. You don't just throw something like that away if you really love someone..." Her voice trailed off after realizing the mistake she'd made. "Oh my God...I have to go."

"Wait! Where are you going?" Rumor called after her.

Cameron ignored her as she jogged up the stairs and went back to the VIP room. She was hoping to run into O' Zone so she could tell him she was about to leave, but she didn't see him.

Zeus was still entranced with the crowd on the dance floor.

Cameron paused, and when she looked closer she noticed he was actually staring down some light-skinned chick dancing on a dark-brown guy. There was envy in his wide eyes as he watched the two grind against each other underneath the flashing colorful lighting.

Cameron was immediately touched by the love in the 6"5 man's dark eyes. It instantly made her think about Jude and all they'd been through together. *How could I be so stupid to throw away what we worked so hard to build? What the hell was I thinking? What is wrong with me?*

A busty redbone rudely brushed past Cameron and entered the VIP. Her rude ass didn't even have enough respect to apologize after bumping into Cam. Her interest in Zeus had made her completely forget to use her manners.

"Hey baby. You want some company?" the impolite woman asked Zeus.

"Bitch, get the fuck away from me right now," Zeus snarled. "I really ain't in the mood."

Cameron cracked a smirk. *Serves her rude ass right.*

All of a sudden, O' Zone stepped inside the VIP room. Wrapping his arm around Cam, he turned towards Zeus. "What's up, big Z? You tryin' to hit up Follies tonight?" he asked.

The cute but impolite redbone stood to her feet, walked over to O' Zone and slipped her arm around his waist. Since Zeus wasn't giving her any of his time she figured she would get it from O' Zone. Hoes would do anything for some attention.

Zeus obliviously didn't hear the question since he was too busy gazing at his lady friend. Finally fed up with watching, he stood to his feet and walked out the VIP room.

"Zeus?" O' Zone called out after him. "Aye, Zeus?"

"What's wrong with him?" Rumor asked after walking up.

O' Zone shrugged. "Fuck it. Shit, ya'll ready to roll out?"

"I actually have to go," Cameron suddenly said, before walking off.

"Hol' up. Where you goin' boo?" O' Zone asked.

"Cam?!" Rumor shouted after her.

Cameron didn't bother responding as she hurried out the club. She sucked in fresh air the moment she was outside. The pill had her feeling hot and clammy. Tears burned her eyes as she walked hastily towards a parked cab.

24

Cameron stumbled inside her home, and completely ignored Elyse when she tried to talk to her. The drugs caused her to have tunnel vision. She desperately wanted them out of her system.

After locking herself inside her master bathroom, Cameron staggered towards the toilet and dropped to her knees. She then stuck her finger so far down her throat that her stiletto nail touched her tonsils. Vomit instantly shot up her esophagus before splashing into the toilet bowl.

What the hell did I take, Cameron asked herself. Half of the drugs she consumed she didn't even know the names of. Xanax. Adderall. Ecstasy. They all seemed the damn same.

Cameron wiped the saliva off her mouth with her wrist and struggled to her feet. She then turned the shower on cold, stripped naked, and climbed inside.

Tears streamed down her cheeks as she sobbed hysterically. She ran trembling fingers through her hair, and allowed the icy water to run over her body. Grabbing the bar of Caress from the soap dish, Cameron began to aggressively scrub the scent of O' Zone off her. However, it seemed like the harder she tried to wash away her sins the more flashbacks invaded her mind. Images of him grabbing her thighs and sucking on her nipples haunted her unmercifully.

What is happening to me?

After scrubbing her skin until it was damn near raw, Cameron climbed out the shower, and into the empty king-sized platform bed.

Jude joined her in the bed minutes after sleep consumed her. He'd paid Elyse, and sent her on her way and now it was just them.

Jude wrapped his arm around Cam as if their conversation from earlier never occurred. She smelled and felt so good beside him. For a moment he'd completely forgotten about the video on Instagram.

Cameron stirred softly when she felt Jude snuggle closer. "I'm sorry," she whispered. "For everything..."

Jude kissed the nape of her neck. His warm breath tickled her skin. "Shit's gotta change, babe," he admitted in a low tone. "We're growin' apart and I ain't feelin' it...I can't lose you, Cam."

Cameron intertwined her fingers in his. "You won't...I'm here..."

"For now...and then tomorrow you'll be back runnin' the streets with ole' girl," Jude expressed. "You gotta life of ya own. I dig that. But what I'm not feelin' is the change in you. It's like you a completely different person. I mean, I don't get it. I thought Cali would make us closer—I thought puttin' a ring on ya finger would show you how serious a nigga really is. But it didn't," he said. "Tell me how I can make this shit right. What am I doing wrong?"

A single tear slid out of Cameron's right eye, and dissolved on her pillow. "It's not you...it's me that's fucking up..."

***

The following morning Jude sat a small plate of sliced fruit on Justin's highchair tray. Sometimes the toddler ate his food and sometimes he made a mess of it.

Jude was just about to look for something to eat when he heard Cam's cellphone chime. It lay temptingly on the kitchen island counter, beckoning for him to be nosey. Closing the refrigerator's door, Jude padded over to her cellphone and picked it up. Cameron's phone required a password in order to gain access, but he had that shit memorized by heart. There were no secrets in their relationships—until lately.

Jude had never been the insecure type, but lately he did have his doubts. He frowned the minute he saw O' Zone's name pop up. Allowing his curiosity to get the best of him, he opened the text message. It read: *Why you dip out the club like that last night? You done got da dick now and said fuck me huh*?

Jude's heart felt like it had dropped to the pit of his stomach. He had to read the brief message three or four more times to make sure his eyes weren't deceiving him. Rage and grief boiled over in him when O' Zone sent a second message that asked Cam if she were still going to be in his music video.

Just then Cameron sauntered into kitchen, toweling off her hair. She wore an oversized white t-shirt.

Jude squeezed her iPhone so tightly in his hand that it threatened to crack at any given moment. Holding it up, he said, "That nigga O' Zone...you fucked him?" His voice was unusually calm, and the seriousness in his tone caused Cam to tense up.

Cam stopped drying off her hair. Her gaze darted from her cellphone to Jude's angry expression. "I—uh…I…"

"*DID YOU FUCK THIS NIGGA*?!" Jude barked.

"Yes!" Cameron cried.

Disappointment and fury washed over him. Without warning, he launched the iPhone at the dry wall, causing it to crack instantly. Justin immediately began wailing after the loud boom, but unfortunately Elyse wasn't there to console him.

"I knew it was something different about you!" Jude hollered. It felt like his heart had been impaled with a sword. Nothing hurt worse than discovering the love of his life had guiltlessly lied down with another nigga.

"Jude, I'm sorry!" Cameron sobbed.

Jude nodded his head in agreement. His face was beet red with anger. "Yeah, you right. You are a sorry ass mufucka. I can't believe you!" he yelled. "I'm out here tryin' to do the best I can for yo' selfish ass and this is the thanks I get?!" Tears pooled in his rage-filled eyes, but he would be damned if he went out crying like a bitch.

"Jude…I…I can't find the words to tell you how sorry I am," Cameron said. "I fucked up. I was so busy trying to find myself, and all I found was trouble."

Jude shook his head in disgust. "I can't believe I ever thought ya ass would be wife material."

Cameron reached for Jude but he moved away from her. "So this what got you runnin' the streets? The nigga that's makin' you wanna stay out at all times of the night like you ain't gotta family? That's what you want? Some fuckin' joke?! Huh?! 'Cuz that's all the fuck you gon' be to him!"

"Jude, please let me explain—"

"Ain't shit to explain. You foul as fuck. You had a real nigga and now you lost him..." With that said, Jude walked out the kitchen.

Cameron anxiously followed behind. They both ignored Justin's high-pitched wailing. "Jude, don't put this all on me!" she yelled after him. "Since you asked me to marry you in Cleveland, I've been feeling like you're forcing me to be what you want me to be!"

Jude turned on his heel and rounded on her. "How the fuck I been forcin' you to do anything?!"

"All you want me to do is stay home, raise our son, cook, clean, and fuck."

Jude scoffed. "And you could barely do two out of those five," he retorted. "Everything I do is for you and Justin! You don't know what all the fuck I go through. You don't know what all I'm sacrificin', but I'm doin' it because I love you! I love our son! I love our family!" he said. "There ain't a bitch in the world that can substitute that." Jude shook his head. "It just fucks me up that you don't feel the same..."

Cameron tried to grab Jude's arm, but he snatched away from her. After collecting his car keys, Jude stormed out the front door, leaving Cam alone with her overwhelming thoughts. Justin's piercing hollers were beginning to give her a headache, and she could barely think straight.

What the hell have I done, Cameron asked herself. There was no way she could let Jude walk out of her life.

***

As soon as Jude hopped inside his BMW 335is, he called up Essence. "Where you at?" he asked the minute she answered her phone.

"At home, doing a little studying. Why? What's up?" she asked suspiciously. Essence wasn't expecting to hear from Jude again since he was supposedly a soon-to-be-married man.

Jude hung up the phone without so much as a response. Twenty minutes later he pulled into her apartment complex. He was an emotional wreck, and he felt the only way he could fix it was by getting his dick wet.

Jude parked crookedly, jumped out his whip, and walked swiftly to Essence's door. When she finally answered he pulled her 5"6 frame close, and eagerly crushed his lips against hers.

Essence's body melted into his at once. She wrapped her toned arms around his neck and pulled him inside her apartment. His fiancé was pushed to the back of both their minds. Essence wanted Jude, he wanted her, and that was all the incentive they needed to have sex.

Jude backed Essence against the foyer wall, and anxiously undid her jeans. She hurriedly pulled the pocket tank over her head, revealing her bare breasts.

Jude rubbed her hot pussy through the fabric of her jeans as he popped one of her hardened nipples in his mouth.

"*Oooh*," Essence moaned. She was both surprised and turned on by his aggression. She couldn't wait for him to take his anger out inside of her.

Jude lifted her up, and she wrapped her legs around his waist. "Where's ya room?" he asked in a hoarse tone.

"At the end of the hallway on the right," she quickly answered. Essence had only dreamt about this moment. *Fuck his fiancé*, she told herself. *If she knew what I knew she'd be trying to hold onto him even more.*

Jude carried her inside her small bedroom, and delicately placed her body on the queen sized Woodhaven bed. The mattress squeaked after the added weight.

Essence promptly unbuttoned Jude's jeans. She was so anxious to feel him deep inside. Her pussy throbbed in her panties—

"Hold up. Hold up," Jude stopped her. She was just about to pull his jeans down.

"What's wrong?" Essence asked, clearly puzzled.

Jude plopped down onto the edge of her bed with his back facing her. "Yo, I can't even do this shit," he confessed. "I thought I could—and I want to—no doubt about it...but I just can't."

Essence was lost. "Huh? I'm so confused."

Jude stood to his feet, and planted a soft kiss on her forehead. Essence deserved more than a revenge fuck. She deserved love, compassion, and respect...but he just couldn't be the one to give it to her.

"I know...," Jude said. "And that's my bad. You don't deserve to be dragged into my bullshit." After fixing his clothes, he walked out of her apartment.

25

After the brief encounter with Essence, Jude decided to get up with King at a popular downtown bar. For the first time, King was solo dolo. The posse who usually followed him around like a herd of bodyguards were nowhere in sight—which was out of the ordinary especially considering the tragedy at his crib. King was currently on a mission to find the motherfuckers who shot his place up. With all the clout and pull he had in the city it'd only be a matter of time before he got some much deserved revenge.

Jude joined King at the bar and ordered a double shot of Remy with no ice.

"Damn...lookin' like somebody havin' a rough day, huh?" King said. He was nursing a beer and a shot of Hen. Once in a while he liked to enjoy some solitude. It offered him time to think and gather his thoughts. Being a boss could be stressful at times.

Jude released a deep sigh. "You have no idea," he said. "Just found out my girl slept with another nigga."

King whistled dramatically. "Shit," he shook his head. "I'd pull the strap out on my bitch if she did that shit. She knows not to try a nigga."

Jude took a sip of his drink. Although he was tempted, he would never put his hands on a female.

"Man, ya'll mufuckas young though," King told him. "Ya'll just kids for real. Ya'll gon' have plenty more fuck ups. It's a just a matter of it bein' worth stickin' it out. You heard me?" He turned towards Jude. "You know how many bitches I done ran up in since the day I said 'I do'? I done got damn lost count. But wifey still ride for a nigga. And you wanna know why?"

"'Cuz she scared to leave ya ass," Jude joked.

"That too," King agreed. "But it's 'cuz she ain't gon' find a nigga realer than me," he chuckled. "My point is people fuck up. If mufuckas don't make mistakes they won't learn any lessons in life. Dig? And don't front like you ain't gotcha share of side pieces too, pretty boy."

Jude took another sip of his drink. "I ain't never stepped out on my girl in all the time we've been together. I could've," he added. "I *should've*—"

"Nah, 'cuz what would that have solved? Nigga, that tit for tat shit juvenile, bruh," King said. "If you really love this broad—and I know you do—you gon' make the shit work. 'Cuz you only find real love once, blood. You can believe that."

Jude sighed dejectedly. "I don't know what the hell is wrong, man...I don't know how to fix this shit. I don't even know if I wanna, real talk."

"You just salty, right now. You'll bounce back," King told him. "Look, I'ma bless ya pockets with a lil' somethin' after this deal goes through tomorrow, and I want you to take some time for yaself. I want you to take ya girl somewhere nice—out the country. Fuck the states." He patted Jude on the shoulder. "Put the past in the past, man. I can look at her and tell she's a good girl. You gotta keep it thuggin'. Nothin's perfect."

Jude thought about what Cameron had said earlier

about him forcing her to be what he wanted. *Is that really how she feels?*

"So do you even know the nigga she fucked?" King asked.

***

This a thousand dollar pair of shoes and U.O.E.N.O it...

This a thousand dollar cup of lean and U.O.E.N.O it...

This a half a million dollar car, U.O.E.N.O it...

I came up from bottom, U.O.E.N.O it...

Jude nodded his head towards a small crowd that had gathered on the dance floor. As usual, fans were flocking to the popular music artist for a chance to get a picture or even an autograph. Surprisingly, Zeus wasn't 'chaperoning' O' Zone for the evening. Instead he had a body guard with him that was of equal stature as Zeus.

"There go that nigga right there," Jude said. There was so much hatred in his eyes as he looked at O' Zone. He didn't even want to imagine him having his hands all over Cameron.

This time around, King was practically twenty deep. He never frequented too many places alone because there were too many haters patiently waiting to catch him slipping.

King gave one of his goons a knowing look. They were used to communicating silently. It came with the job.

Jude watched as King's boy slid O' Zone's bodyguard a small knot of cash in order to scram.

Afterward, they played the waiting game until the moment they could catch his ass alone. When O' Zone finally did step outside to smoke and clear his mind, King, Jude, and his crew followed suit.

O' Zone stood in the parking lot, shielding his hand over the L to light it. At first he didn't even notice the group of guys surrounding him. Initially, he thought he was about to be robbed. O' Zone wondered why they were so deep if they were only planning to rob him. *Something told me not to bring my ass out here without security*, he thought to himself. However, he figured what was the worst that could happen.

O' Zone looked around suspiciously at the gang of guys closing in. They formed a tight circle around him, and from the looks on their face it was obvious that they meant business.

Jude stepped between two niggas and approached O' Zone slowly. The more he rocked with King the more the older man started to rub off on him. His good guy rep was slowly disappearing, and a monster was taking its place instead.

"What's happenin'?" O' Zone asked. He was starting to panic a little, but he didn't want to let it show. After all, they would only feed on his weakness.

Jude pulled his NIKE vintage hoodie off and tossed it to the ground. "Nigga, I'm finna whup ya ass. That's what's happenin'."

O' Zone looked at all the men surrounding him. Based on their serious expressions they weren't letting him go without a fight. They didn't give a damn about his celebrity status.

O' Zone looked back at Jude. It was then that he finally recognized him. "Man, this about that bitch, ain't it?"

WHAP!

Jude hit O' Zone directly in the chin. The blow sent him crashing to the concrete. The lighter and blunt instantly flew from his hands, landing several feet away. It felt like the wind had been knocked out of him, and for a few seconds he lay on the ground stunned and dazed.

"Get ya mothafuckin' ass up, nigga," Jude demanded while holding his hands up in a fighting stance.

O' Zone looked up at Jude like he was crazy. "So this what this shit comes down to, man? We gon' fight over a bitch like some mufuckin' niggas in high school?"

King aimed his KAP-40 at O' Zone. "Get yo' punk ass up and fight. Or you can die like a mufuckin' coward," he said. "All that bullshit you spit in them songs, but you ain't tryin' to throw no hands...Bitch ass nigga."

O' Zone hastily scurried to his feet. He would be damned if he had his dignity insulted. He was a man about his. Holding up his hands, O' Zone and Jude squared up.

Without warning, O' Zone dived at Jude and attempted to grapple him. It wasn't shit for Jude to sidestep him, and hit him in the side of the head with a brutal punch. O' Zone accidentally fell into the crowd of men surrounding him. They heartlessly shoved him back in the center of the circle where Jude hit him with two vicious blows to the face.

Unable to hang, O' Zone dropped to the ground pathetically. *I can't believe Cam slept with this weak ass nigga*, he thought.

Jude didn't give O' Zone time to recuperate before he grabbed him up and put him a savage headlock. "Nigga, if you ever call, text, or even *think* about Cameron again I'ma kill ya ass! And that's on life!"

King slowly stepped in the center of the circle. A Cohiba Behike cigar hung out the corner of his mouth. He leaned down and looked at O' Zone in disgust. "And then I'ma have my young niggas bury ya body so ya lil' fans can't have a proper burial." With that said, he snatched O' Zone's solid gold diamond chain off his neck. It was his most prized possession.

Jude tossed O' Zone onto the ground like a ragdoll after he'd beaten up and humiliated the rapper. As quickly as they came they dispersed, leaving him lying in the parking lot bloody and bruised.

"Nigga, fuck you and that weak ass hoe!" O' Zone shouted after Jude. He spat a tooth out onto the ground. Blood oozed from his busted mouth and nose. "That's why every time you hit that shit she gon' be thinkin' 'bout me makin' dat pussy cream."

Jude instantly turned on his heel, preparing to break O' Zone off again. However, King quickly stopped him. "Fuck that nigga. He's a done deal," he said. "Besides, we got other unfinished business…"

26

"Don't you think he's had enough?" Jude asked. His knuckles were slightly sore and bruised after whupping O' Zone's ass, but his pain seemed minimal when he stared at a dying Vado.

The cuts and nicks on his bare ivory skin looked as if they were getting infected. He also smelled horribly. As a matter of fact, Jude smelled Vado before they even walked in the room where King was holding him hostage.

"That's why I brought you in here," King answered. He then pulled out his gun and handed it to Jude. "After tonight, you know I'll ride for you...but will you do the same for a nigga?"

Jude looked at the gun in King's outstretched hand. "I ain't a killer...," he said.

King chuckled. "...After seein' you in action tonight, you definitely a mufuckin' killer, dawg...," he said. "I only fuck with killers..." Without hesitation, he pointed the gun at Vado and squeezed the trigger.

POP!

***

The following morning Cameron noticed that Jude didn't return. She couldn't say that she was all too surprised. She wanted to call him, apologize, and beg for him to come home but she knew he needed his space. Who wouldn't after finding out they'd just been cheated on?

Cameron sat on the living room with her son as she watched him play with a Fisher-Price tool set. Justin had made the living room his own personal play room.

On the spur of the moment, Cameron burst out crying hysterically. Justin immediately stopped what he was doing and stared at his mother sobbing. He was confused because he was too young to understand her pain and guilt.

Cameron pulled him close and held him tight. "I love you so much," she cried. "Mommy, really loves you…I'm so sorry…"

***

Rumor lumbered into the bathroom that morning. After running cool water over her face to wake herself up, she opened the medicine cabinet. There were several bottles of prescription pills lined up on the top shelf.

Rumor popped a pill from each prescription bottle and slammed the medicine cabinet close. Same ritual but a different day. Every day for the rest of her life she would have to take the 6-drug regimen to stay healthy.

Life's a bitch and then you die.

After bathing and eating breakfast she went to check on Calix. He was beginning to look like he was losing weight. The whites of his eyes were slowly turning yellow, and he appeared sickly.

Rumor leaned down and removed the duct tape so that he could speak.

"Rumor," he croaked out. "I'm…dying…baby…"

Rumor rolled her eyes and covered his mouth again with the duct tape. "Serves your trifling ass right," she said before leaving. She didn't even bother feeding him that morning.

***

Jude looked out his hotel room's window at the city. The foggy, gray sky hinted that a rainstorm was approaching shortly. Instead of going back home he had gotten a room at the Atlanta Marriott Marquis. Understandably, he needed time for himself to deliberate.

Jude thought back to King's wise words: *"If you really love this broad—and I know you do—you gon' make the shit work. 'Cuz you only find real love once, blood."*

***

Rumor sat at the vanity as she called Cameron for the fourth time that evening. She hadn't talked to her girl since the night they were at Reign Night club, and she was beginning to grow worried. She didn't know if Cameron just didn't want to be bothered with her or if she just needed some alone time.

After drawing her own conclusion, Rumor hung up the phone and tried to put herself in the moneymaking mind frame. It was only Thursday, but Persuasions was fairly busy that evening. When she emerged from the dressing room, she looked around at the crowd and tried to see who was worth approaching.

Out of nowhere, someone grabbed Rumor's wrist from behind.

The moment she turned around she nearly threw up at the sight of Roxie standing in front of her. There was a smug expression on her pretty dark brown face.

Rumor snatched away from her sister in disgust.

"You just love popping up announced, huh?" she asked.

"Well, it seems like this is the only place I can catch you at," Roxie said. She looked stunning in an Aztec print Bodycon dress with nude single sole heels. Her long, wavy mane hung over her shoulders. Rumor and Roxie's resemblance was undeniable.

Rumor started to walk off but Roxie grabbed her wrist. "Sis, we need to talk. You can't ignore me forever."

"We don't have shit to talk about," Rumor snarled. "Go kill yaself."

Roxie anxiously pulled out a few crumpled up bills. "Well, fine. Gimme a lap dance then. Since I've got the money you've got the time. I know how this shit works."

"Bitch, don't get slapped trying to be cute," Rumor warned her.

"You have the right to be mad at me...but don't take it out on Calix. After all, I was the one making all the advances, to keep it real."

Without thinking, Rumor slapped the shit out of Roxie. A few passing people stopped and looked at the two sisters standing in the middle of the floor. They were expecting a fist fight, but Roxie didn't even bother hitting Rumor back.

"I deserved that," she said.

Rumor stepped so close to her sister's face that their noses were practically touching. "No, bitch. You *got* what you deserved," she spat.

TAT! TAT! TAT! TAT! TAT! TAT! TAT! TAT!

The sound of an HK mp5 going off was followed by high-pitched screams.

Rumor grabbed Roxie and dropped to the floor after the sound of loud gunshots. Tables toppled over, glasses shattered, and piercing screams drowned out the strip club's music.

Four masked criminals dressed in all black stormed inside Persuasion. "Everybody get on the mufuckin' ground!"

Two of the goons ransacked the building, snatching money off the dancers, and floors before shoving it inside black trash bags. One of the criminals held the bartender at gunpoint while forcing her to hand over all the money.

Rumor watched in horror as the obvious leader stomped a guy out for not handing over his Versace chain. It was at that very moment when her life flashed before her eyes. All of her reckless decision-making had led her straight into this situation.

"Bitch, come up off that bracelet." One of the gunmen pointed his gun at Roxie. He eyed her diamond tennis bracelet through the eye slits in his ski mask.

"Fuck you! Kiss my ass!" Roxie hissed. "I'm not giving you shit!"

Roxie's boldness instantly set the gunmen off. Ruthlessly, he snatched her to her feet by her hair.

Rumor quickly jumped to her feet. "Don't fucking touch her—"

WHAM!

The butt of a Desert Eagle slammed into Rumor's temple instantly knocking her unconscious.

***

Jude laid on the king size bed inside his junior suite, scrolling through videos and photos in his cellphone's gallery. He'd watched the one from Cali several times.

"Scream that shit, bay."

Cameron tossed her hands in the air. "WOOOOO! I'm in Cali, bitches!"

Jude cracked a smirk when he thought about all the good times they'd shared. He could hear King's voice in the back of his mind saying, *"It's a just a matter of it bein' worth stickin' it out."*

***

"I don't want to go to no damn hospital!" Rumor yelled. "I just want to go home!"

A couple EMTs struggled with trying to get her onto the stretcher. "But ma'am it's best for you to go to the hospital to make sure you don't have a concussion. An injury to the head can be very serious—"

"Rumor, just let them look at you!" Roxie begged. There were tears in her light brown eyes, and she was missing her precious diamond tennis bracelet. The four masked criminals had robbed Persuasion, and its customers of all their money and valuables. Business would surely decline after tonight's tragic events.

Rumor shoved a female EMT, and jumped off the stretcher. She nearly lost her balance when she landed on her feet. Half-swaying, half-running, she hurried to her candy red 2013 Lexus. Roxie was hot on her heels.

"Sis, wait!" she called out.

With trembling fingers, Rumor hit the unlock button and hopped inside.

Roxie quickly grabbed the door before Rumor could close it. "Wait, I...I just wanted to tell you I'm sorry...And thank you for what you did in there. I know you probably hate my fucking guts—and I don't blame you, but I appreciate you sticking up for me," she said. "You probably saved my life..."

Rumor wiped away her tears with the back of her hand. "It doesn't matter. You might as well be dead..." She grabbed the door handle and slammed it shut.

Roxie was left standing confused in the parking lot as she watched her sister pull off. She had no idea what Rumor meant by that statement.

Rumor drove to nowhere in particular. She'd told the EMTs she simply wanted to go home, but the thought of being there only saddened her. There was so much history and pain...not to mention Calix being tied up in the garage.

Tears blurred Rumor's vision to the point where it became difficult to drive. She was on 75 when she pulled over on the side of the freeway and climbed out. Her head throbbed in pain, but seeking medical attention was the last thing on her mind. Rumor hated hospitals. It was the very place she'd found out she was HIV positive.

Tears cascaded down Rumor's chocolate cheeks

as she leaned against her car. The moment she found out it felt like her entire world was crashing down. Her future looked blank. She was only twenty-six and living with such a heavy burden.

Calix swore he didn't know who he'd gotten it from, and he seemed genuinely hurt and guilty for giving it to Rumor. He'd begged her to stay and even proposed because he felt they could work it out. And she believed it too...up until his recent infidelity...and with his sister of all people.

Overwhelmed with emotions, Rumor pulled out her cellphone and dialed the only person she could think to call.

Cameron answered on the third ring.

"Thank you for finally answering," Rumor said.

Cameron sighed. "Sorry, but I'm just going through some things right now—"

"*You*?!" Rumor repeated. "Tell me about it. Persuasion just got robbed tonight by some people."

"Get the hell out of here!"

Rumor wiped her nose and sniffled. "That ain't the worst part though," she whispered. "I'm standing on the freeway now...There's an eighteen-wheeler approaching...and I'm thinking about jumping in front of it..."

27

"Woah! Woah! Are you serious—You don't wanna do that, Rumor!" Cameron said, thinking about Tiffany. She'd already lost one good friend to suicide, and she didn't want to lose another.

Rumor broke down crying on the other of the phone. "But I'm dying, Cameron...," she choked out. "And not just physically. Mentally too...I feel fucking hopeless. I feel like a got damn walking zombie, Cam. Like this is the end of my life—this is how my fucking chapter closes—"

"But it doesn't end there," Cameron told her. "It's only a mere obstacle. Don't take the weak way out, Rumor. You're stronger than this. I know you are..."

Rumor sniffled. "I don't know what to do."

"You love your man?" Cameron unexpectedly asked her.

"Very much," Rumor confessed.

"Then go home. Call that man. And get back what you worked hard for," Cameron said. "Seven years is a long time. It's not worth throwing away if it really means something..." she paused. "I wish I would've taken my own advice."

Rumor mulled over Cameron's words. "Thank you," she finally said. "I'll sleep on it..."

"Go home, Rumor."

"Good night, Cameron..."

***

The following morning, Cameron jumped off the couch the minute she heard the front door to her home open. A smile spread across her face when she saw Jude step inside. However, it vanished just as quickly because she didn't know if he was staying or going.

Jude tossed his keys on a coat hanger and walked past Cameron without speaking.

"Jude, talk to me..."

He turned around and faced ger. "You know you completely obliterated my trust. You know that shit, right?"

Cameron sighed deeply, opened her mouth to say something, but closed it. In her head, she'd rehearsed a bunch of things to say when he finally came home. Yet now he was here and she couldn't think of a single thing to say. "Jude...I'm sorry. I made a mistake."

"Yeah...that you did, baby girl," he agreed. "But its gon' take more than some lame ass rapper to make me fall out of love witchu."

A smile tugged at the corner of Cameron's lips. "So does this mean you forgive me?" she asked hopefully.

Jude slowly made his way over towards Cam. He was a few inches taller than her so he had to look down to gaze into her eyes. "No," he said flatly. "But I can put it behind me and move forward...startin' with makin' you my wife."

***

The sweet aroma of breakfast wafted through the air. Pancakes, sausage, scrambled eggs with cheese, golden hash browns, and croissants lined the dining room table. A pitcher of freshly squeezed orange juice sat in the center.

Beyoncé's "1+1" played softly on the audio system.

After preparing the table for a hearty breakfast, Rumor gradually made her way to the garage. This was the first time in a long time that she was actually sober. When she flicked the light switch on she saw Calix lying feebly on the ground. He looked weaker than ever.

Rumor knelt down, and brought a sharp-edged knife close to him. Muffled screams came from Calix as he instantly tensed up. He calmed down when he noticed she was cutting him free.

If I ain't got something…I don't give a damn…

'Cause I got it with you…

I don't know much about algebra…but I know…

One plus one equals two…

After finally setting Calix free Rumor stood to her feet, and walked back into the dining room. For a few minutes, he simply sat on the ground dumbfounded.

Calix took his time standing to his feet. His muscles were stiff and sore from lying on the hard concrete for days on end. After a good stretch he limped out the garage. He had uttered so many threats and promises to kill Rumor when he was free, but now that he was that was the furthest thing on his mind. Sitting trapped in a garage for weeks had given him a lot to think about.

Calix joined Rumor at the dining room table,

piled breakfast on a porcelain plate, and proceeded to eat like an inmate after being released from prison.

"I'm really sorry, Rumor...," he said, breaking the silence.

Rumor paused but didn't respond. A simple apology would never return things to normal...but at least it was a start.

***

Jude dropped over twenty-two thousand dollars on a trip to Santorini, Greece for a wedding and a three-night accommodation at *La Maltese*. Instead of having a huge wedding, Cam and Jude decided to have a private ceremony at the five-star hotel. There were flowers, champagne, and even a photographer so they could take pictures.

The beautiful Greek island was unlike anything Cameron had ever experienced. The view from the hotel offered magnificent scenery. Expensive furniture, antiques, oriental rugs, a grand piano, and chandeliers were only a few of the luxuries offered. The place felt more like a residence or getaway than it did a hotel. *La Maltese* provided a romantic, elegant setting that Cameron had only ever dreamt about.

Cam felt like a queen being pampered as she stood on the 250 square-meter veranda overlooking the Aegean Sea. She wore a $2000 Carine Gilson satin robe, and the 14k white gold diamond ring glistened on her finger.

"This is...absolutely...unbelievable...," Cameron whispered, looking out at the sea.

Jude looked stylish and handsome in a charcoal Waraire Boswell suit. His dreads were pulled back and his edges were tapered to perfection. Sitting on the plump outdoor sofa, he poured them each a generous amount of *Gerovassiliou Malagousia*—a Greek sweet red wine.

Cameron sauntered over to the sofa and took a seat beside her new husband. The veranda was so quiet, peaceful, and exotic. There was even a crystal blue pool which sat on the furthest end of the veranda.

"Let's make a toast," Jude said, handing her a wine glass.

"What are we toasting to?" Cameron asked.

Jude lightly clinked his glass against hers. "To a future filled with laughs and happiness as husband and wife."

They took a small sip of their wine.

"I cannot believe we're married," Cameron said breathlessly. "I never even thought I'd be here...with you...right now. This is just crazy."

Jude kissed the back of her hand. "Believe it, baby..."

Cameron hesitated because she really didn't want to ruin the mood, yet her curiosity was getting the best of her. "Jude, I told myself I wouldn't hound you about it...but now I really have to know...," she began. "How can you afford all this?"

Jude released a breath. He knew it was coming sooner or later. "Come on, Cam. Don't fuck up the mood with all the questions and shit," he said. The agitation was evident in his voice.

"Is it legal?" Cameron asked.

Jude sucked his teeth and stood to his feet. Leaving Cameron alone on the veranda he headed back to their suite. Cameron hastily followed behind him. She was just about to harass him for answers until she saw the white rose petals sprinkled on the floor, leading to the plush king size bed. On top of it was a long red velvet box and an envelope with a card enclosed.

Jude took a seat on the bed and pulled Cameron into his lap. Handing her the red velvet box he prompted her to open it.

Cameron drew in a deep breath as she slowly lifted the lid. Inside was a 1 ½ carat round-cut diamond necklace. Just that quick she'd forgotten about her suspicious. "Jude...I...this..."

"Let me put it on for you," he said. After securing the $3,000 piece of jewelry around Cameron's neck he handed her the rectangular envelope.

Delicately, Cam opened it and pulled out the greeting card. Several Benjamin Franklins fell out the card and landed on her lap before she read the bold, cursive lettering.

To my wife,

Doing absolutely nothing with you means absolutely everything to me.

"Sweet," Cameron smiled. She turned around and looked at Jude. "Thank you—but this doesn't mean you're off the hook. Jude, I still need answers. I deserve them," she said. "I could've died at that cookout..."

"Cam, you really workin' hard to kill the vibe. Ain't you?"

"Jude...I'm serious," Cameron stressed. "Is it legal?"

Jude sighed in frustration and ran his hand over his dreads. "You really want the truth?"

"Of course..."

"Nah. Nothing about what I'm doing is legal," he finally confessed. "I been lyin' from the jump."

Cameron closed her eyes and allowed the pain to settle in. "Well...What is it that you do?" she asked calmly.

"Bay, I really don't wanna get into the details—"

"Tell me!"

"Aight. I work for an advanced car theft ring transporting stolen cars to Port Newark-Elizabeth."

Her mouth curved into a frown. She wasn't expecting that response at all. "I think telling me it was drugs would've been better," she said. "That sounds like some deep shit."

Jude shook his head. He was disappointed in himself, but the money was so easy and convenient. It also felt good to be surrounded by a team of niggas that had his back. With Jerrell gone it was comforting to know that he had someone to look out for him.

"It is deep—"

"Well, you need to get out," Cameron said with finality.

"It ain't that easy, babe."

"What kinda example would this set for our son?"

"What kinda example were you setting twirling around a damn pole?" Jude asked sarcastically.

"And you made me stop," Cameron reminded him. "Do you remember that?"

"But you still went behind my back. You remember that?"

"Don't turn this on me," Cameron said, climbed off his lap and standing to her feet. "This is about you." She tossed a hundred dollar bill at Jude. "Conspiracy." She tossed another. "Theft." Then another. "Fraud...Prison"

"Cam, I just can't—"

"I can't believe you lied to me, Jude."

Jude stood to his feet. "You knew it all along, Cam. Be real. You just chose to ignore the shit."

"How could you put me and Justin in harm's way like that?" she asked. "You knew what you were doing was wrong but you still brought us to that man's home—"

Jude pulled Cameron back onto his lap as he sat on the edge of the bed. "I would never let shit happen to you or Justin. That's on everything I love," he promised. "I would die for ya'll, straight up."

"Then leave that shit alone," Cameron told him. "Get a regular nine to five—I'll get one too. We can do this together—the right way." She picked up his hand and kissed his wedding band. "We're married now. We gotta family. We can no longer make reckless decisions...I know that now…"

Jude rubbed his chin and thought about her encouraging words. King wouldn't be all too pleased with him trying to back out the car ring, and sadly Jude was still uninformed about the strict "No Resignation Policy".

"Fuck it, you want me out I'm out," Jude finally told her. "I'ma let 'em know as soon as we get back to the states. My family is what's more important."

Cameron kissed Jude's forehead. "Thank you…"

Jude reclined in the bed, pulling Cameron down on top of him. "You mad?" he asked in a low tone.

"I'm a little disappointed that you lied to me…but if you can get past my mistakes I can get past yours."

Jude gently rolled on top of Cameron. "That's all I need to know, babe…" He leaned down and ran his wet tongue along her chin up to her lips before sliding it inside.

Cameron moaned as he kissed her passionately. His erection pressed against the silk fabric covering her hot pussy.

"You gon' be mine forever?" Jude asked. It was his favorite question.

"Yes, baby. For however long you want me," she whispered.

"I'ma want you for as long as I live…and shit, even after that…" He moved her panties to side and slipped a finger inside. He curled it upward and played with her G-Spot. He had memorized every area on her body that stimulated her.

"*Mmm.*" Cameron moaned when he slicked his wet finger over her clit and softly massaged it. He then sucked off her juices, stuck his finger inside her mouth, and allowed her to suck off any remains.

Jude's dick strained against his dress pants as Cameron seductively swirled her tongue around his digit. When he could no longer take it, he slid out of his dress clothes.

Cameron eyed his butter pecan-colored chest. There was a small scar from where Silk had shot him a few years ago. They had been through so much together.

After freeing himself of all his clothing, Jude grabbed Cam's left leg, brought her foot to his mouth, and nibbled on her heel. He then ran his tongue slowly up her leg and inner thigh. Her body trembled as he took his time. When he reached her sopping pussy, he curled his tongue and proceeded to suck on her pearl.

"I love how this pussy tastes. I can live off eatin' this shit...," he whispered.

Cameron's back arched. She bit down on her bottom lip and grabbed a handful of Jude's dreadlocks. Her cheeks grew warmer as sensation overwhelmed her.

Jude's long, pink tongue looked like an ocean's waves as he slowly licked her pussy. He made passionate groaning noises while he devoured her which really turned Cam on. When it began to feel too good to the point where it was unbearable, she tried to inch away.

However, Jude firmly grabbed her plump ass and pulled her towards his face. "Don't run from it," he said before sliding his tongue inside of her. In a vigorous motion, he moved her hips back and forth so that he was making love to her with his tongue.

"Shit! Jude, you're going to make me cum doing that!" Cameron moaned.

"Unh-unh. Not yet," he smiled, climbing between her legs.

Cam's cheeks flushed when he entered her. It felt like pure ecstasy...better than any drug she could ever consume. "I'm addicted to you...," she murmured.

Jude kissed her deeply while gradually rotating his hips inside her. "Don't you ever give a nigga my pussy again. You hear me?"

Cameron encased her bottom lip and nodded her head.

Jude sat in an upright position and placed both of Cameron's legs over his shoulders. Grabbing one of her breasts, he filled her with gentle, even strokes. "That nigga fucked you like this?" he asked.

Cameron shook her head. The sex was so good that she could barely talk. Jude had her breathless.

He took his time with each calculated thrust, making sure to hit her spot repeatedly until he felt her juices drench his dick.

Cameron's leg shook uncontrollably. Tears welled up in her eyes, and her cheeks were bright pink.

Jude placed a hand on her flat tummy and used it to guide his deep strokes. She had soaked up the sheets with her wetness, but he wouldn't be satisfied until he made her cum two more times.

"Tell me it's mine…"

"It's yours!" Cameron exclaimed. "It'll always be, baby."

"Damn right…"

28

Aso swaggered into King's office that evening looking more like his old self. After weeks of letting himself go he'd finally cleaned up, shaved his stubble, and got a haircut. Tank's death had temporarily put him in commission, but now he was back and ready to get to the money.

"What's up?" he greeted King. "You wanted to holla at me?"

King placed his pen down and made a pyramid with his large hands. "How you feelin'?" he asked, genuinely concerned. Aso may've acted like a pussy at times, but he fucked with the kid. He'd seen potential in him since the day he let him join his team.

"Man, I'm straight. Everybody sweatin' me like a nigga finna kill himself or some shit," Aso complained.

"Well, you did just lose ya brotha. I know how that shit can be. I done lost *two*." King held up his fingers to indicate the number.

"Like I said, I'm good," Aso reassured him. Although he was slowly healing, Tank was still a sensitive subject.

King nodded his head in understanding. "Well, I'm glad to hear you bouncin' back. That's real good. 'Cuz I'ma need you to take over for Tank...I really don't trust nobody else with that position. Plus he's ya bro' so it's only fair I come to you before anyone else. You think you can get ya hands dirty? 'Cuz Tank was doing big boy work. Not that petty shit I'm paying you to do—"

"I knew what he did," Aso cut King off. "And I'm down for whatever. Shit, you already know. My brother gone now...Niggas thought I ain't give a fuck about shit then...well, I really don't give a damn about shit now. I'm twice as nonchalant."

King smiled, pleased with Aso's change of attitude. No longer did he view him as a weakling. He was talking like a big man now. "In that case this job'll be perfect for you."

"It's whatever," Aso agreed.

Just then a 6"6, 250-pound man stepped into the vast, luxurious office. His skin was black as coal and there was an intimidating expression on his face. Because of his occupation he was soulless.

"Meet ya new patna, Axel..."

***

It wasn't even noon yet, and Ericka Matthews was prepared to stir up some trouble. Rihanna's *"Jump"* bumped through the speakers of her Camry as she took her time driving down Ms. Patterson's street.

Ericka had driven up and down the older woman's street so many times that she now had her schedule down pact. She knew what time Ms. Patterson went to the local convenience store to buy scratch offs, and even what time she went to church.

As expected, Ms. Patterson's 2013 Lincoln MKZ wasn't parked in the driveway of her cottage home.

"This old bitch is so fucking predictable," Ericka laughed. After killing the engine she stepped out, and walked briskly across the street.

Ms. Patterson's neighbor eyed Ericka suspiciously as he cut his front lawn.

Ericka forced a fake smile, and even waved for good measure, but the white man didn't return the greeting.

"Racist fuck," she muttered.

As if she paid the bills or had her name on the lease, Ericka proceeded to go through Ms. Patterson's mail. She was hoping to find something that had Jude's new address on it. *He has life fucked up if he thinks he's about get away from me*, she told herself. Flipping through various envelopes she prayed to find a letter addressed from him.

A slow smile crept across Ericka's heart-shaped pink lips. "Bingo..."

***

"Thanks for meeting me, man." Jude dapped up King, and took a seat next to him at the bar.

Essence didn't bother greeting him or even looking in his direction for that matter. Understandably, she didn't want to be bothered with someone that led her on only to let her down.

Jude thought about saying something to her—maybe apologizing for playing with her feelings—but he figured it was best to just not say anything.

"You know it ain't shit. I could've used a drink anyway," King said. This time he was solo dolo. With a five-seven tucked in his waist he wasn't worried too much about anything. "So what that wedding was looking like? Was it everything you thought it would be, man?"

"It was straight. Everything went good," Jude answered.

King nodded his head. "Good. Good. That's the shit I like to hear. So what you had wanted to kick to me?"

Essence slammed a Heineken down in front of Jude before walking off. Both men noticed her disposition but chose not to comment on it.

"I want out," Jude finally said. "I can't fuck with this shit no more, man."

Disappointment resonated in the pit of King's stomach. Just hearing Jude say those words left a bad taste in his mouth. He wasn't expecting for Jude to say that, but he couldn't say he was all too surprised. Jude was a good guy...but the fact of the matter was once you were in, you were in. There was no getting out.

"You sure you wanna do that?" King casually asked, taking a swig of his beer. He didn't bother warning Jude about his deadly decision to leave The Ring. He was under the impression that Aso had already told him what was up, but apparently that wasn't the case. Or maybe it was but Jude expected to get special treatment.

"I'm positive," Jude said, completely oblivious to his fate. "Man, I gotta wife now...a kid...a family. I can't be doin' this shit no more. The money is good and all. Don't get me wrong...but I gotta put the fam first," he explained. "They're all I got. You know where I'm comin' from?"

King scoffed and nodded his head. "Oh, I get it...I get it loud and clear..."

Jude dapped up King, thinking everything was

cool. "Good lookin', man. I was lightweight sweatin' comin' to you 'bout this, but I'm glad you understand."

King didn't respond. He simply nodded his head in false comprehension.

After dapping up King one final time, Jude headed towards the exit. He didn't bother touching the complimentary beverage. When he reached the door he looked back at Essence. She stood at the cash register. When she looked over her shoulder at him, and saw him watching her she quickly looked away. Without another word, Jude exited the bar not even realizing the situation he'd just walked into.

King took another sip of his beer, and then pulled out his cellphone.

Aso answered on the second ring. "What's good, boss man?"

"It's lookin' like you got your first job," King told him. "What I need for you to do is teach that naïve ass cousin of yours a lesson. You heard me? Now don't kill him," he quickly added. "I don't wanna take him out the game just yet...All I need is for you to hit him where it hurts. You think you can do that?"

Aso was driving through downtown Atlanta while talking to King on the phone. He was on his way to the strip club to fuck off, but his boss' proposition sounded a lot more interesting.

"Yeah," he agreed with a sneaky smile on his face. "I can definitely do that..." After disconnecting the call, Aso made a quick detour.

29

Cameron emerged from the master bathroom wearing a nude pajama shorts set. Her short hair was lightly damp from the shower she'd just taken, and her soft skin smelled of Japanese Cherry Blossom.

Jude had called her ten minutes ago telling her that he was on his way, and she was trying to wait up for him. Unfortunately, she was completely unaware of the two men standing outside her home.

Without warning, Axel kicked in the front door! The scenario was much like the one that had occurred at Mitch's home in New Jersey.

Cameron jumped, and Justin began hollering after the loud boom. Her heart instantly dropped to the pit of her stomach. At first she didn't understand what was happening. Fear kept her feet planted to the carpet even though her brain told her to run.

The sound of heavy footsteps grew closer, and Cam knew that the invaders were heading upstairs.

Justin!

Acting quickly, Cameron ran out the bedroom—and straight into Axel's closed fist. He had hit her so hard that her skull instantly cracked. She was unconscious before she even hit the floor.

***

When Jude pulled up to his house and saw his front door wide open panic immediately washed over him. After hastily parking, he raced inside his home. Justin's cries were the first thing he heard.

Jude's heart hammered in his chest as he sprinted upstairs. Thankfully, he found Justin unharmed inside his crib, but when he ran in his bedroom there was no trace of Cameron. He ran through the entire house, and even checked outside before concluding that she was gone.

***

Cameron smelled the scent of liquor on Aso's breath before he even opened his mouth. Her eyelids fluttered as she struggled to gain consciousness. Her head throbbed in agony, and for a few seconds she saw double.

Aso lay on top of Cameron in a stained, rickety, old wooden bed. They were inside of a decrepit, abandoned shack out in Lithonia, Georgia. The dilapidated home was located on a long, winding country road surrounded by a mass of trees and tall, unkempt grass.

Aso had stumbled upon the abandoned house one afternoon while driving, smoking, and listening to music. He figured it would be the perfect destination to have his way with Cameron. Aso had even told Axel to go ahead on his way, claiming that he could handle it from there.

"I been waitin' patiently for you to be conscious for this shit," Aso said. She could feel his hard dick pressing against her thigh, and it made her sick to her stomach.

"Where am I?" Cameron asked, taking in her surroundings. "Why did you bring me here?!" She tried to push Aso off and run, but he grabbed the back of her collar, and snatched her backwards. The material literally choked her after he grabbed her up.

Aso manhandled Cameron by tossing her into a nearby wall. She slammed against it and fell onto the creaking floors. A water bug scurried away after she almost landed on top of it.

"You know what I noticed about you?" Aso said, unfastening his jeans. "You like to tease...And then you got the nerve to be stuck up ass fuck like you never saw a nigga eyeing you. I hate bitches like that." He pulled his dick through the opening of his boxers. Heartlessly, he urinated on Cameron like a dog to its special tree.

She groaned in pain as she struggled to get up. The blow to her head had weakened her tremendously.

All of a sudden, Aso stomped onto Cam's hand using all of his strength.

"*AAAAAHHHHHHH!*" Her bloodcurdling scream bounced off the decaying walls of the room. It was the same hand she'd broken after getting jumped by Pure Seduction a few years ago.

Cameron sobbed hysterically as she cradled her injured hand. Her pajamas and hair were soaked in Aso's piss. Tears streamed down her dirt-stained face. She couldn't figure out what hurt most, her hand or her throbbing skull.

Aso was so ruthless with his assault. He didn't stop after peeing on her and breaking her hand. He whupped Cameron's ass like she was a guy in the streets. By the time he finished with her, her face was barely recognizable. Blood soaked her nude pajamas, and she could hardly move an inch. Pleased that he'd weakened

Cam to the point of immobility, Aso stripped Cam naked on the gritty floor and violated her. He didn't give a damn about the blood or the fact she reeked of his urine.

"You ain't shit, bitch." Aso hocked up a loogie and spat it in Cam's face while choking her with both his hands. His thrusts were deep, painful, and uncoordinated. "When ya'll punk ass son grow up he ain't gon' be shit either."

"Fuck...you," Cameron weakly forced out. Her face reddened from being choked. She hoped Aso would put her out of her misery.

Aso cackled. "Nah, you don't fuck me, baby girl." He pulled out and flipped Cam over onto her stomach. "I fuck you...," Without warning, he entered her dry, virgin asshole.

"*AHH—*"

Aso covered Cameron's mouth to keep her from screaming. With his free hand he held her in a headlock position while fucking her from behind. Her ass felt like it was on fire as her skin tore from the painful penetration.

Aso bit her shoulder until he drew blood. He wanted to hurt Cam so badly since he couldn't physically hurt Jude. By the time he finished with Cameron, his cousin would finally see just how much he hated his guts. Jude had totally underestimated the power of jealousy and envy. As a matter of fact, he'd been downright blind to it.

"You been teasin' me since the day I met you," Aso breathed in her ear. "You been wantin' this shit as much as I did. Didn't you, bitch?"

Cameron's muffled screams were the only

response he received.

"Fuck! I'm 'bout to cum!" Aso quickly stood to his feet and jerked his dick over Cameron. Warm semen splattered over her bloody and bruised body. She'd never felt more humiliated. Death seemed a better alternative.

However, instead of killing Cameron, Aso left her alone inside the abandoned shack. Cameron lay motionless on the floor as she listened to the sound of his car pull off. Street walkers were treated with more respect. When she tried to move it only caused more pain so for an hour she simply lay outstretched on the cold, dirty floor.

Cameron wanted to cry, but strangely, no tears would fall. It was as if she were void of all emotions. After lying on the floor for what felt like an eternity, Cam finally picked herself up and limped towards her clothing. Some parts of her body were so sore that they felt numb. Her left eye was swollen shut, and her nose was twisted at an awkward angle. Aso had really went in on her.

Cameron stepped out the empty, run-down home looking worse than Emmett Till during his open casket funeral. Her bloodstained pajamas made her look like a character straight out *Nightmare on Elm Street*. Only Freddy Kruegar wasn't the villain. Instead it was a cynical thug by the name of Abel Soden, also known as Aso.

Taking slow awkward steps, Cameron gradually made her way up Rock Springs Road barefoot. Oddly enough, she didn't feel anything. Initially, she felt disgusted, hurt, and confused...but now her mind was like a blank canvas.

Cameron wondered if this was how Rumor felt when she was tempted to commit suicide.

Staring straight ahead with an expressionless look on her face, Cameron staggered past an old graveyard. Each step she took caused major discomfort. The smell of urine coupled with sweat filled her nostrils. Aso's cum had dried, causing it to harden and stick to her skin.

Cameron wouldn't wish this type of treatment on her worst enemy. She knew without a doubt that it'd be a while before she used the bathroom the same.

After walking for what felt like forever, Cameron made it to Evan Mills Road. She didn't know where the hell she was or which direction to go. A hunch prompted her to turn left so she did. Trees surrounded her on either side, and she walked along the curb to keep from being swallowed up by the woods.

Suddenly, a '98 Jeep Grand Cherokee pulled alongside Cameron as she traipsed up the dark street barefoot.

30

The passenger window to the Jeep rolled down. "Hey, you need a ride or somethin', Miss Lady?" a deep, raspy voice shouted out.

Cameron ignored the help offered. As a matter of fact, it was like she didn't even see or hear him. She seemingly had tunnel vision as she walked to no destination in particular.

"*Hello*?! Are you deaf or something?" the stranger asked.

No response.

"Well, fuck you then, trash ass hoe!"

SCCCCRRRRR!

The driver skirted off in haste after insulting Cam, but she didn't care. After tonight, she just didn't give a damn about anything. She didn't feel anything. She hurt...but she wasn't in pain. Her feet were sore...but she was numb all over.

Cameron finally saw a Citgo when she reached the intersection of Evans Mills Road and Mall Parkway. The station was filled with a couple cars. A strung out white woman leaned against the building, begging for spare change or a cigarette.

Everyone immediately stopped what they were doing when they saw Cameron walk up. Her left eye was swollen shut, her cheeks were puffy and bruised, and two speed knots had quickly formed on her forehead. Blood dripped from her busted mouth down her chin.

A cigarette dropped out of a man's mouth when he saw the battered women limp past him. A middle-aged woman covered her mouth in shock. Cameron pretended she didn't see the many stares as she traipsed down the walk of shame.

Using what little strength she had left, Cam opened the station's door and hobbled to the counter. "Do you...have a phone...I can use?" she asked the clerk through a swollen mouth.

***

Jude slammed his fist repeatedly on Rumor's front door. His heart beat so fast that it felt like it would explode out his chest. It didn't take rocket science to figure out something was wrong. It was unlike Cam to just up and bounce like that, especially with Justin home alone.

After knocking on Rumor's door for what felt like hours she finally opened it, but barely. "Do you know what time it is?" she asked with an attitude. She had no real legitimate reason to dislike Jude.

"Did you talk to Cameron? Do you know where she is?" There was urgency in Jude's voice as he berated her with questions.

"I haven't talked to her all day," Rumor said.

"Everything aight?" Calix asked, coming up behind Rumor. He sized Jude up wondering why he was on his girlfriend's doorstep.

It was as if the whole garage ordeal had never happened. The damage was still there, but they loved one another too much to leave. Aside from that, they were bound by a mutual sickness that plagued. It would take some time for their wounds to heal, but with patience anything was possible.

"Ya'll been up each other's ass since the day we moved here, and now you don't know where the fuck she at?" Jude yelled. He was taking his frustrations out on Rumor. "Bitch, I swear to God if you lying—"

"Aye! Aye!" Calix moved Rumor out the way and stepped up to Jude. Just a few weeks ago he was ready to kill Rumor, but he would be damned if he stood by and let Jude insult his girl.

Just then Jude's cellphone began ringing, breaking up the tense moment. Jude was just about to steal on Calix, so he should've considered himself saved by the bell.

The unrecognizable number had a 770 area code. "Hello?" Jude answered.

"Jude...I need you to come and get me..."

Jude breathed a sigh of relief when he heard Cameron's voice.

"Is that her?" Rumor asked in concern. "Is everything okay?"

Jude ignored her question since she was of no help anyway. He ran back to his car and hopped inside. "Tell me where you're at, baby," he said calmly.

Jude drove over 80 mph on the freeway, and he didn't slow down until he reached exit 74. Justin sat asleep inside his car seat, thankfully able to rest through all the madness.

When Jude reached the Citgo he jumped out the car so fast that he almost forgot to put the gears into park. The moment he saw Cameron standing in front of the store he wanted to knock out the first motherfucker that he laid his eyes on—which just so happened to be an older African man standing beside her.

"Who the fuck did this shit, Cam?" Jude's voice cracked as he spoke. He was so overwhelmed with emotions seeing his girl like that. He almost didn't even recognize her because of how badly she'd been beaten. "YOU DID THIS SHIT, MOTHAFUCKA?!" Jude yelled, grabbing the guy up by the collar of his shirt.

"No, he didn't, Jude! Let him go!" Cameron pleaded. Her voice came out muffled, and she could barely communicate clearly.

Jude hesitantly released his hold on the clerk who was polite enough to wait with Cameron. Returning his attention back to his injured wife, Jude lifted Cam and carried her to the truck. The stench of Aso's urine reeked from her skin, and her blood smeared his clothing, but Jude didn't give a damn about that. All he cared about was her health and safety.

Jude carefully placed Cameron in the passenger, circled the truck, and hopped into the driver's side. "Tell me who the fuck did this shit, man?" Tears spilled over his lower lids. "I'ma kill the mothafucka with my bare hands and that's on everything, Cam." He looked down at her bloodstained hands trembling uncontrollably in her lap, and it nearly killed him inside.

Cameron remained silent as she stared straight ahead.

"Don't just sit there quiet. Tell me who did this shit!"

No response.

Accepting that Cameron wasn't going to give him an answer, he wiped his tears with the back of his hand, and snatched the gears into Drive.

***

A cracked skull, fractured ribs, broken hand and nose, and internal bleeding and tearing were only a few of the injuries Cameron had sustained at the hands of Aso. She still didn't understand why he'd treated her in such a way. It was like she could feel his hatred as he penetrated her roughly. Cameron would never be the same after tonight.

Jude held her hand while he sat at her bedside. His thoughts were all over the place, and he'd even given himself a headache. He couldn't figure out why Cameron chose to protect the person who had hurt her. It didn't make any sense.

Jude licked his dry lips. "Cam...please...Tell me who did this to you," he pled. "A nigga ain't gon' be able to sleep until I know. You gotta tell me, bay. Please...I'm fuckin' beggin' you. This shit is killin' me, man. Who did this?"

Cameron looked straight ahead. She was unsure of how he'd react, and if he did something reckless she'd never forgive herself.

Jude kissed the back of her hand. "Please, Cam...I deserve to know...," he said through clenched teeth.

Her head and torso were bandaged. She wore a cast

on her hand and forearm, and her nose was covered with a splint. In a low tone she finally said, "Aso..."

Jude froze in place after hearing his cousin's name. He wanted to believe he'd misheard Cameron, but she would never lie about such a thing. Anger built up inside of him and made his blood boil. Overwhelmed with fury, Jude hopped out his seat, causing the chair to topple over. He then raced out the door.

"Jude!" Cameron called after him.

Jude didn't stop until he made it to the parking lot. When he reached Cam's Audi q7, he placed a hand against it, and tried to catch his breath. His emotions were a wreck. "I'ma snap this mothafucka's neck," Jude promised himself. After hopping inside the truck he called Aso's cell number.

Surprisingly, his treacherous cousin answered. "What's good, cuz?" he asked casually.

The fact that Aso spoke as if everything was okay pissed Jude off even more. It made him feel as if he were taunting him. "For yo' sake you better hope I never find yo' ass, nigga!"

Aso cackled in amusement. "Bruh, that shit was A-one," he teased. "How the fuck she keep that thang so tight?"

Jude's grip tightened on the steering wheel. Gritting his teeth in anger, he envisioned himself strangling Aso. "I'ma rip ya mothafuckin' eyes out, nigga," Jude threatened.

"Whoa! Whoa! You mad at the wrong nigga

anyway, cuz. I just carried out ya boy King's orders. He was the one who wanted this shit to go down."

"The fuck you talkin' 'bout?"

CLICK!

Aso disconnected the call.

"*FUCK*!" Jude screamed. He punched the center of his steering wheel, causing the horn to blare.

Jude thought about him and King's earlier conversation. Everything seemed cool, and King seemed understanding towards his decision to leave The Ring. Jude couldn't figure out why his boss would want to hurt Cam...but he was definitely about to get to the bottom of it. Snatching the gears into drive, Jude headed to the Warehouse.

31

Jude boldly burst into King's office. His fists were clenched tightly, and he was ready for answers, and if he didn't get them he'd beat them out of King.

"Man, what the fuck is wrong witchu?" Jude yelled.

King grabbed a pistol out the holster underneath his desk, and aimed it at Jude. "Nah, nigga what the fuck is wrong witchu bustin' in my office like you crazy?"

Jude stopped in his tracks when he saw the loaded gun.

"Sit yo' mothafuckin' ass down," King demanded.

Jude's nostrils flared wildly. Apart of him still wanted to take his chances by fighting the older man.

King cocked the gun.

Rethinking his actions, Jude hesitantly took a seat behind the desk. His rage-filled gaze settled on King's light brown eyes.

"Like I told you before, without consequences there ain't no lessons to be learned, ya dig? And you had to learn a valuable mufuckin' lesson."

Jude's jaw muscle tensed. "Are you telling me you had Cameron...," he paused, not even wanting to use the word 'rape'. "You had Asu hurt my wife 'cuz I wanted out..."

King chuckled. "Ain't no such as out, blood," he said.

If looks could kill Jude would've murdered King a thousand times over.

King stood to his feet, rounded the desk, and sat on the edge of it beside Jude. "I know how you feelin'. You wanna murk a nigga right now, huh? But look at it like this, I did you a favor. I'm giving you a second chance— somethin' I don't do for most niggas, 'cuz I fucks with you. I respect you. But I also gotta business to run," he explained.

Jude didn't respond as he stared daggers at King. If it wasn't for the gun in his hand he would've attacked him without a second thought.

King chuckled. "I know what you thinkin'. You probably wanna kill me. Maybe you even thinkin' about runnin' and takin' ya family with you," he said. "But I guarantee I will find you...and then I will kill everything you love before killin' you. That shit I did to Vado, it was nothin'. I can and *will* put yo' ass through the worst pain imaginable. You heard me?"

Jude swallowed the lump that had formed in his dry throat, but he didn't respond. His fists were still clenched, and he was tempted to pummel the man who'd had Cameron attacked.

"You made a mistake—it ain't a big dead...But you had to learn from it," King told him. "Now you wanna sit here, huff and puff, and be mad at the world? Or do you wanna get this money with me? It's up to you, patna?" He extended his hand in hopes that Jude would make the right decision and shake it.

Jude wanted revenge, plain and simple. He

would've loved to take the pistol from King and put a bullet between his eyes. He anticipated seeing Aso take his last breath after hurting Cameron. He absolutely despised them for hurting his girl. Besides that, he hated the person he was letting the business turn him into.

Fleeing the state seemed like a great option. However, Jude knew that he could only run for so long. He was only twenty-four. He was just one person, and King had a whole army of niggas. He was a powerful man with powerful connections. Jude really didn't see any other way around his dilemma.

Swallowing his pride, Jude shook King's hand...fighting the urge to spit in his face as well. At the end of the day, he had to do what he had to protect his family.

King smiled, pleased with his protégée's wise choice. "I knew you were a smart guy," he said. "I really ain't wanna have to kill you. You're too big of an asset."

***

Aso had just rolled out of bed, and stepped into the bathroom for his morning pee. Suffering from a hangover, he felt no remorse for the vicious assault he'd inflicted on Cameron. He was so jealous about Jude coming down to Atlanta, and stealing his shine that he couldn't wait to take it out on Cameron.

Aso reclined his head, and allowed his urine to splash into the toilet bowl—

BOOM!

The sound of his front door flying off the hinges

caused Aso to accidentally urinate on the toilet seat and floor. "Fuck was that?" Before he could investigate several armed police officers rushed inside the bathroom and forced him to get down. He felt like an absolute fool as he knelt in his own urine while being read his rights.

"Abel Soden, you have the right to remain silent. Anything you say or do can be held against you in the court of law."

"What did I do?" Aso asked as he was handcuffed.

"You are being charged with the murder of Lana Princeton—"

"Man, get the fuck out of here!" Aso screamed in anger.

Apparently, Lana's parents had filed a missing person's report. When they finally found her decomposing body in a dumpster all fingers pointed to Aso. He never thought he'd have to pay for that sin. However, he would be damned if he went down alone.

***

Jude stepped into Cameron's hospital room the following morning carrying a bouquet of gerbera daisies and a Get Well Soon card. He hadn't slept all night, and the weariness was evident from the look on his face. However, Jude tried his best to force a smile.

"Good morning," Cameron greeted. She was starting to feel a little better with her son by her side. He reminded her that she had made something worth living for.

Jude placed the bouquet of flowers on the counter,

and kissed Cameron on the forehead. "How do you feel?" he asked.

"A little sore...but I'm alive...," she paused. "I prayed that you wouldn't do anything stupid after you stormed out of here last night."

Jude grimaced. Inadvertently, she'd saved lives with her prayer. "You my wife," he said. "I would die for you...kill for you...Cam, I would do whatever to protect you."

Cameron reached over and touched Jude's hand. "I know..."

Jude kissed each finger on her hand and held it against his warm cheek. "I really love you, baby...and I wish I could tell you I don't know why this happened to you—but that shit would be a lie.

Cameron's hand went limp. "What do you mean? You know why Aso did this to me?" Her voice cracked as emotions washed over her.

Jude dropped his head in shame. "I done got into some shit...and I don't know how to get myself out of it," he admitted. "I can't stop fuckin' with this car shit—I wish I could be the legit husband you want but I can't. And I don't wanna lie to you anymore. If you don't wanna fuck with me no more, I understand. The last thing I want is to be the reason something happens to you or Justin."

Cameron tilted Jude's chin toward her so that she could look in his eyes. "I'm not going anywhere," she told him. "We've been through worse than this together. I'm staying right here...with you. Whatever you go through, I'ma go through it with you because we're in this together."

Jude felt relieved to hear her response. He smiled and kissed the back of her hand. "I—"

His sentence was immediately cut off after an army of police officers barged inside. Cameron was completely shocked as she watched them grab and arrest Jude. "Wait—what's going on?!" she asked. Cam struggled to climb out the bed even though her body was in so much pain.

"Jude Patterson, you're being charged with the murder of Lana Wright—"

"Murder?!" Cam repeated skeptically. "What murder?"

The officers led Jude out the room. He couldn't even look at her because he was so disappointed and embarrassed. Up until today Jude hadn't even thought about the day he'd helped Aso get rid of her body.

"Jude, please tell me you don't have anything to do with a murder," Cameron begged him. Tears slid down her cheeks as she hobbled down the hallway after them.

"I didn't kill anybody, Cam!" Jude tossed over his shoulder.

"Jude?!" Cameron screamed after him. *JUDE*?!"

32

The thought of prison had made Aso panic so badly that he opted to turn over King's entire operation in exchange for immunity. Abandoning his dignity and nobility, he ratted out everyone and everything without regards to the consequences of being a snitch. He even lied to the investigators by telling them that Jude was in fact the one who had killed Lana, and he was simply forced to help dispose of her body.

Aso had gone out like a total bitch. His freedom was way more important to him than the money King paid him to work, and keep his mouth closed. He was worse than Frank Lucas as he tossed government names out. Unfortunately, Aso was unaware that he'd have to sleep in the bed he lay in.

***

Fortunately, King was able to pull some strings to get Jude and Aso out on a reasonable bail. He had a lot of pull in Fulton County, and of course money talked. However, there would still be a trial, and Jude and Aso were still capable of facing some serious time for Lana's murder.

King had even gone out of his way to pay for all Cameron's medical bills in hopes that it'd be water under the bridge. He never intended for it to go as far as it did, but a valuable lesson had to be taught. Disloyalty was not an option. And he had to remind motherfuckers of that shit by using Aso as a perfect example.

With a little money, King was able to get Aso's

statements tossed in the trash. Even with all his snitching and backstabbing he was unable to bring King's million-dollar empire down. By the time King finished with Aso he would've wished he was rotting away in prison.

***

Rumor stared at the name flashing across her cellphone's screen as she sat on the edge of her bed. Calix was asleep after a bland sex session. They were taking it day by day, but the mission wasn't an easy one by far.

Calix knew he was never going to find a girl to put up with his shit, and still love him regardless of his faults. And it went both ways. Calix was the only one who could tolerate and handle Rumor's crazy antics. They were perfect for each other even though they were individually flawed.

Breathing a sigh of irritation, Rumor tiptoed to the master bathroom and answered the call.

"What do you want, little girl?" she asked agitatedly.

"What did you mean?" Roxie suddenly asked. "Back at Persuasion in the parking lot...what did you mean I may as well be dead?"

Rumor paused and thought of a response. She wasn't ready to blurt out and tell her that Calix had HIV, so instead she said, "No one can escape the consequences of their choices..."

"Huh?" Roxie asked in puzzlement. The wise words had flown completely over her head.

"Go and get yourself tested...," Rumor said before

hanging up.

***

Jude stood emotionless as he stared at Aso bound to the same chair that had Vado was tied to. He'd been stripped of the majority of his clothes, and King had let his young niggas have a field day on his ass. Aso had been beaten so badly that it was a miracle he was even still breathing.

King handed Jude his Five-Seven. "You still think you ain't a killer?" he asked.

Jude carefully took the loaded weapon from him. His heart beat rapidly in his chest. He'd never done anything as intense in his entire life. Tomorrow was his birthday, but celebrating it was the furthest thing on his mind, considering all the events that led up to this point.

Jude slowly lifted the gun, and aimed it at Aso. He was his cousin—his family—but Jude would never be able to forgive him for hurting Cam. Although, King was the one who ordered the attack it felt good to get revenge on someone—anyone.

Perspiration formed on Jude's forehead, and the bridge of his nose.

Aso's head hung low. He was barely conscious. It was because of his snake ass that Jude could possibly go back to prison for a murder he hadn't even committed.

Images of Cameron's bloodied hands trembling in her lap instantly set him off. Without remorse, he squeezed the trigger. A single bullet tore through Aso's skull, killing him instantly.

Jude's chest heaved up and down. He looked like someone coming up for air after swimming underwater. He'd never actually taken someone's life. With a steady hand, he lowered the gun. Jude's heart hammered inside his chest.

Satisfied, King patted Jude on the back, and took the gun from him. After today he knew Jude's loyalty was genuine.

Re-holstering his gun, King said said, "You keep workin' hard and maybe one day you can hold the business down after I retire," he told him. "I could use a protégée. Shit, ain't no way I'd have my daughter runnin' it."

Jude tried to open his mouth to say something, but the shock of killing his cousin had rendered him speechless.

King chuckled. He remembered the first time he'd taken a life. He looked just as stunned as Jude. "Come on. Let's a have a drink. You look like you could use one, bruh."

***

The following morning Cameron was finally released from the hospital. When she and Jude got home they noticed a letter had been slid under their door.

Jude had been really brief with her about the murder he was convicted of, but she couldn't beat an explanation out of him. If he said that he didn't kill anyone then she had no choice but to believe and trust him. However, the thought of him possibly going to prison would surely put a strain on their marriage.

Jude bent down and retrieved the letter as Cameron proceeded to get settled in. When she checked her cellphone she noticed she had a dozen missed texts from Rumor checking to see if she were okay.

Cameron decided to hit her back later. For now, she simply wanted to pop a pain pill and relax. The house didn't feel as homely as it did in the beginning, mainly because so much had happened.

"I'm going to put Justin to bed. Can you run a warm bath for me?" Cameron asked Jude over her shoulder. He hadn't said a single word since he picked up the letter.

Jude didn't respond to her request. He was too busy re-reading over the brief, hastily scribbled note:

Roses are red. Violets are blue…

Your ass thought you could run, but guess who found you…

PART 5 IS NOW AVAILABLE!

JADED PUBLICATIONS Presents

5

CAMERON

JADE JONES

OTHER AMAZING SERIES BY THIS AUTHOR!

http://amzn.to/1pvtJ16